ALL THE TIME IN THE WORLD
A Time Traveller's Tale

A Science Fiction, Action Adventure, Novella
By Michael John Siddall.
Copyright © 2014

M&E&B BOOKS UK

This novel is dedicated, as always,
with much love to Elijah and Benjamin, my two
beautiful children who I love and adore with all my
heart.

Text copyright © Michael J Siddall 2014
Cover Art copyright © Elijah Siddall 2025

Proofreader Elijah Siddall

All rights reserved

The moral right of the author and illustrator has been asserted

Condition of sale

This book is sold subject to the condition that it shall not, by way of trade or otherwise, be lent, resold, hired out or otherwise circulated without the author's prior written consent in any form of binding or cover other than that in which it is published and without a similar condition including this condition being imposed on the subsequent purchaser.

*"...Time exists. Its function is to stop everything happening all at once.
It ticks away slowly like a river flowing gently from the past, through the present to the future, so if a significant new event is introduced into the normal flow of Time, it will branch off, creating a new version of the future, hopefully without causing a destructive Time Paradox..."*

Chapter 1

It was a late afternoon in early April of 1912, seasonably cold for the time of year and beginning to snow. The breath of passengers passing me by was visible, wafting up into the air and I turned suddenly, looking out to sea from the promenade deck. It glistened. Ominously it was dotted with icebergs, even though only small ones the size of houses.

My attention wandered as I cast my eyes back over the shadowed faces of the passengers. They seemed thin-faced people with greedy eyes, well-heeled, dressed in expensive clothes and draped in jewelry. I stared at one man, meeting his gaze, but he slid away and it struck me that he looked tired, possibly ill.

Suddenly, chunks of ice rumbled against the sides of the ship, shaking it violently as the stars looked down upon us. *We've only been sailing for a few hours, but it seems like a lifetime,* I thought, watching a nearby iceberg shed more ice. Huge chunks tumbled against each other, falling into the sea with a great creak and crash amid roiling waters, and I held onto the silver handrail tightly. *I must leave before it's too late. No one believes what I've said anyway.*

Staring up at the silver moon I shivered from the cold, despite my heavy fur lined coat. *God help them all. Most are going to die tonight and I don't want to be here at the end and be one of them. Luckily, I can escape. However, fifteen hundred will die, including E. J. Smith, the captain of this great liner. He's a proud man, a brave man – but a stupid one. He should have listened to me.*

More chunks of ice slammed into the ship, shaking her. I jumped as if slapped; turning my head and a beautiful woman caught my gaze. Her name was Mary Astor and her plump cheeks were red with cold, but she smiled at me kindly. "Don't worry about the ice hitting us, this ship is unsinkable," she whispered softly with confidence, her hair gathered together beneath a hood set with pearls. How wrong she was. *A very rich woman,* I thought, *and one whose husband will die tonight because there aren't enough lifeboats.*

I looked back out to sea and it was calm, almost black in colour and freezing cold. The surface glistened and now there were much larger icebergs to see. *No one can survive out there for more than a few minutes,* I thought. Ironically, all of the people on board had chosen to take the trip to New York feeling completely and utterly safe. *How little they knew and how wrong they were, and how surprised they'll be when we hit the fateful iceberg that sinks us.*

"But this ship is *unsinkable*," they'll whisper, a look of dread on their faces when they realise that it's not.

The hand of God in his Divine Judgment will strike this ship down and sink it on its maiden voyage, and our time is almost up, I thought, turning away from the handrail. I walked back towards the stern, glancing briefly at the faces of all those who would soon lose their lives, and they already looked like lost souls – ghosts. If only they had listened to me.

However, they thought me mad, so why do I feel guilty. I tried to warn them. "When a huge iceberg looms from the dark and is spotted by the lookout at the last moment, don't change your course; hit it head on. If you try to turn the ship to avoid a collision, you'll still strike the iceberg and rip a great hole four hundred feet long below the waterline. And twelve inches of steel plating is no match for thousands of tons of ice," I had said. But would they listen? *No!*

"How can you possibly know what's going to happen?" they had asked me. I told them. They didn't believe me.

"Go away you crazy man," they said. "We aren't going to hit an iceberg and even if we do, we won't sink!"

More loose ice slammed into the ship, shaking her. *I can't afford to stay any longer. I can't help these poor people. Most are doomed.* I carried on walking stern-ward, shaking my head solemnly, feeling great despair. Then I paused to study my own reflection in a porthole, staring at my hair streaked with grey and the deep lines on my face. I felt awful. Desolate. *I can escape a dreadful disaster, but most will not.*

The sun had set hours ago and it was dark, almost pitch black. *Soon there will be the inevitable fateful crash, and the ship will sink to the bottom of the Atlantic Ocean in two hours, where it will lay for many years to come until discovered again. However, I won't go down with the ship. I have a remedy for my plight, an escape route like no other. I tried to warn them. I tried my best, but they wouldn't listen.*

Despite my anxieties and the freezing weather conditions, I felt relaxed, peaceful almost. But only because I knew I could avoid this dreadful situation – a disaster of huge proportions and a tragedy that will live on in infamy for many, many years to come.

Placing my hand into my deep coat pocket, I took out my watch. *Nearly midnight... mere minutes to go,* I thought, staring at the fluorescent dial. I glanced down at the silk napkin that had fallen from my pocket. I picked it up. *Even with this as proof, no one back home will believe me when I tell them where I've just been. My mother won't believe me. Neither will my father, family or friends. God help me, I hardly believe it myself.* I crumpled the napkin to make sure it *was* real. It was of course. I straightened it out again, staring at the blue emblem and neat embroidery, which read: R. M. S. TITANIC. 1912. Yet I wasn't born until 1962 – fifty years after the disaster.

I know, you're asking yourself how this could be... and it's a strange tale to tell. However, it's one that's worth listening to if you have the time. Well, do you? Because I'm a Time Traveller with... all the time in the world!

Chapter 2
LONDON. ENGLAND. PRESENT DAY.

Let me introduce myself. My name is Ben Ward, and I *am* a Time Traveller. The year is 2011 A.D. and I'm forty-nine years old, tall and muscular with dark eyes and greying hair and I'm good looking, but not what you would call handsome. My ears are too small, my crowded teeth are crooked on the bottom, and while it seems I'm a quiet, scholarly man, I'm broad-shouldered, strong, well-coordinated and quick when I need to be. And my adventures began a year ago to the day, when I received a package from a company called *Time Unlimited*. This is what happened next.

...Opening the package, I ran my fingers over the smooth cover of a mail-order catalogue. Normally I never shop by mail order, so it seemed like the hand of fate had redirected the catalogue away from its rightful owner and sent it to me. I looked at it, flicking through its pages. *Do I need anything?* Usually I dump mailers, flyers and free samples immediately without even reading or opening them. However, the parcel had intrigued me simply because it wasn't mine. I know that's wrong, but my curiosity got the better of me.

I walked over to the wall bar to make myself a drink – a Glenlivet on the rocks with a splash of water. Measuring it out I sipped at it and it was good. Then I walked back over to the catalogue, picked it up and sat down on my couch, lifting my legs up to relax. Slowly, I flicked through the pages again. There was everything from carpets and curtains to cars and caravans. I drank some more of my scotch, wandering back over the brightly coloured pages. *I have a nice car*, I thought, *wouldn't have a caravan given me, don't need furniture or carpets, light fittings and fixtures, a washing machine, dishwasher, but ah, I do need a Sat-Nav... that I could use.* I rushed through the pages to the Sat-Nav section. Curiously there was only one, made by a company called *Timeline*, and unlike the rest of the photographs in the catalogue it was in black and white, looking very old.

A simple description below the photograph declared: *A Sat-Nav like no other with special functions and features – availability, one only at a special price of five thousand pounds. It's an extremely high price to pay, but you will not be disappointed. It's a one-of-a-kind, collector's piece.*

I must admit, although staggered by the price, which astounded me, making my eyes bulge, I was still intrigued. I finished my drink and made another, then searched for the appropriate order number. Picking up my mobile phone, I dialed the mail-order department at Time Unlimited. They answered straight away; however, it was so quick that it seemed as if someone was waiting just to take my call. It was *uncannily* fast.

"Yes?" asked a quiet, flat voice at the other end.

"Want to order something," I proclaimed uneasily. The price *was* staggering for something as simple as a Sat-Nav. In fact, it was so expensive that it made my head swim. *I must be mad,* I thought, but I couldn't seem to stop myself from ordering it.

"Is the required article that you wish to purchase on page two hundred of our catalogue?" the voice inquired, again in the same flat tone.

"Why, yes, it is," I said, astonished by the telephonist's clairvoyance. "It's the..."

"Special Order Sat-Nav..." the voice interrupted, drifting away.

That was a bloody good guess, I thought. I drank some more of my scotch, a couple of gulps, and went to look out of my open window. The lights of London winked at me and it was warm outside, even though it was raining heavily. Finally, a softer voice asked for my credit card details and my name and address, which I duly gave. I frowned. *What am I doing? It's a hell of a lot of money to spend on such a trivial item,* I thought. But then again, I couldn't seem to stop myself from giving the required details. It was as if I was hypnotised or something.

I took a strong pull on my scotch, polishing it off, as the voice at the other end of the line announced a 'done deal', and that no money would be refunded if I wasn't a happy camper. Those few words made me feel even worse than I already did, and as the five thousand pounds disappeared from my bank account with the making of a simple 'phone call, the photograph of the Sat-Nav began to fade from view also. Then it was gone completely, right before my eyes. I pinched myself to make sure I wasn't dreaming. I wasn't. I pinched myself again just to make sure. I *was* wide-awake.

The list of offerings in the catalogue had changed now too. There was no mention of a Sat-Nav for sale on any page. Stunned and completely spellbound by what had just happened, I stared at the catalogue. Suddenly, it seemed to close by itself. *It has to be the breeze from the open window,* I supposed. However, this was turning out to be a very strange day indeed.

I chewed gingerly on the inside of my lip, having never heard of a company called *Time Unlimited* before, but I had assumed that the company was a highly respectable department store that would not offer anything they couldn't deliver, should a buyer appear who was interested in one of their products. 'This is nuts,' I said to myself out loud, staring at the catalogue in disbelief, almost certain that I had made a big mistake by ordering anything.

I went to the bar and poured another scotch. This time it was neat. I sipped at it. *This is crazy*, I thought as the scotch worked its way into my head.

I stood up to walk it off, glancing at my watch. 7:00pm. *The store will have closed by now, but I can leave a message on their answering machine, cancelling the order.* I picked up my mobile and rang the number. However, instead of getting an answering machine, the line went dead with a click. I rang the number again. The line was still dead. This was getting stranger by the minute. I dialled my friend, Emma, to make sure the mobile was working okay.

"Hello," the familiar voice answered.

"Hi, it's me, Ben, are you okay? Not heard from you in a while."

There was a pause on the other end of the line. "Yeah, I'm okay," she said, "how about you? We'll have to meet up for a meal and a chat. Long-time no see!"

"Yeah, it's been a while. Been busy this year," I admitted. "Just thought I'd give you a quick call to make sure you're okay, seeing as I haven't heard from you in ages."

"Okay, I'll call you to arrange something, so look after yourself. See you soon!" She sounded happy and in good health.

I must have been working too hard. I must have fallen asleep while drinking the scotch and imagined it all. That has to be it. I'm overworked, overtired and my imagination is playing tricks on me. Sure, the catalogue is real. But the Sat-Nav isn't. I never really rang the order-line. I thought, slipping off to bed quietly.

***

THE NEXT MORNING I was late getting to work. I had scheduled a meeting with my colleagues for 9:00am, at the Court Buildings, only to discover that the clerk had removed our sitting from the docket because of my lateness. As a solution I reset the date for our meeting, two weeks hence, and decided to take a break, because the earliest court date I could get on the docket was in thirty days. I needed a break anyway. Being a lawyer isn't easy work and I was beginning to hallucinate for God's sake!

Anyway, my ongoing case-load wasn't that important. Well, not life or death, so time was not of the essence. It was only a Traffic Offense I was working on, so no one was going to jail or getting a death penalty, and I did need a break. Some time alone.

When you think about it, there is *never* enough time. People are always in a hurry, rushing here and there, and I'm sick and tired of the whole business of having no time to spend on myself, whether it's a second, a minute or even a day. My life to date seems to have been a blur. A blink of the eye. The flap of a butterfly's wing. I wish I had *more* time. I wish. I wish. If I wish hard enough, can I get what I want?

I became a lawyer to make big money and get my name in the papers, besides helping people. However, the legal profession is a quagmire of legislation and regulation that stretches from here to eternity. Judges and lawyers alike don't understand the half of it. The courts are overburdened and slow and can't make sense of it. And frankly, I'm sick of it. The Law as it stands right now is no more than a game, which no longer cares who is innocent or guilty. The highest paid lawyer with the flashiest profile and hard-ball reputation usually wins the case.

There are exceptions, but they're rare. My profession is in a mess and has the worst possible press because we don't police ourselves adequately. And it's all down to how much time we have to do the things we need to do, to make things right. I can tell you honestly that I'm not satisfied with the direction my life is taking, or has been taking for the last five years. Something has to change. But I'm not sure what. However, when I decide what it is that has to change, will I have the time to change it? You see, *everything* is to do with how much time we have.

The past, present and future will collide at some point, I'm sure, and fuse like the crystals in a kaleidoscope. For a time it will even form a pretty picture. Then it will explode into chaos just like our lives. One minute we're on top of the world feeling wonderful, and the next minute our lives dissolve into complete chaos and utter confusion. And it's all down to the effects of time.

Sod it! I spent the rest of the day relaxing. The next day too. Then a parcel arrived for me. I wasn't expecting anything because I'd forgotten about the catalogue incident, but I signed for it anyway, taking delivery out of pure curiosity. Just then, my mobile rang. I picked it up and answered. "Hello," I said in a small voice, inspecting the brown parcel in my other hand.

Wrapped securely in thick Manila paper and tightly bound by layer upon layer of plastic tape, I couldn't even hazard a guess at what it was. "You have received your order today, *yes?*" said a flat voice on the other end of the line. Stunned, I realised it was the same voice I'd spoken to, two nights earlier. I hadn't dreamt the incident after all. I cleared my throat. "Er, yes, thank you," I replied. "Just signed for it now!" There was a long silence. I waited, listening.

"Yes, I know you have," said the voice. There was eerie laughter on the other end of the line. Then it went dead with a click. I rang Time Unlimited back. The line was dead now. *Someone's messing with my head. But how could they know I've just received their parcel unless someone is watching me,* I thought.

I broke open the wrappings quickly. Inside was a small, black leather case engraved with a golden insignia – a thunderbolt passing through the centre of a cloud. Hesitating for a moment, I glanced at my watch. 2:00 pm. I didn't open the case; instead I went to the health club to work out.

When I got there, I spent two hours in the weights' room, one hour on the speed-ball and a further hour on the fighters' heavy bag. I'd boxed as a youngster, fighting out of Sheffield where I was born, and could possibly have been a Golden Gloves champion at an early age, if my interest in law hadn't taken me away to college in London. I still like to keep my hand in though and do a few rounds of sparring each week. However, for the most part, I simply like to work out; stay fit and keep my mind and body sharp. I've done it religiously, ever since my wife Jane was murdered. I always have and always will, because it helps me release the frustration and anger I feel, and also helps me fill my time. See what I mean? It's always about *time*.

It's true to say that I haven't been able to accept Jane's premature death, and can admit that I don't know how to accept it. I had loved her with an intensity that was frightening, and she had loved me the same way, but when I lost her to the hands of a murderer I wanted to take my own life too. I hadn't done so, simply because my two children needed me more than ever, but I had become a grief-stricken recluse, hiding from the world while I mourned my dead wife. However, now I'm slipping back into myself more and more with my growing case-load of work and new social life. And no, there isn't another woman, because no other can make me feel the way Jane did.

After leaving the health club, I went straight home. Well, almost. On the way, I had a flat tyre. Then a flat battery. A stranger waylaid and accosted me, stole my wallet and tried to stab me. Finally the police arrested *me,* throwing me into a cell for defending myself with a tyre iron. I considered it reasonable force, but they didn't. However, I'm the lawyer and I was right, so they had to release me on bail.

When I finally got home it was nearly 9:00 pm. I mixed a scotch with water and retired to the living room, seating myself on the couch, staring out of the window into the lights of the city. They were winking at me again, and after a time I picked up the small leather case delivered that morning. I'd been thinking about it all day and sat staring at the case for a long time, glass in hand. *How special could a Sat-Nav be that costs five grand?*

Just then, my land-line rang, and before I could answer it the answering machine kicked in. "Ben, its mum, how are you feeling today? I spoke to Dr. Aldrich and he said that you'd cancelled your appointment again. Please look after yourself. I don't want your depression getting the better of you. Please call me. I love you so..."

I picked up the receiver before it went dead. "Hi mum. Stop worrying about me so much, I'm a lot better than I was. That's the reason I cancelled the appointment. I need to sort my own head out now. Doctors can only do so much, so stop worrying okay, I'll be fine. Love you. See you soon. *Night!*"

She said goodnight and the line went dead. I put the receiver back on the bracket and picked up the leather case. Crossing the room to the bar, I polished off my drink in one big swallow and poured another, toasting myself solemnly in the mirror. Then I drank it before opening the case to examine the contents. I was exhausted, but curious to see what I'd got for my money.

When I finally took the Sat-Nav out of the case I was impressed. It was a nice bit of kit with a small square screen that was anti-glare. I read the basic start-up instructions. On the main-frame screen it had been programmed with: *Places of Interest, Favourite Places, Fuel* and *Hospitals*, besides several other useful features. On the second screen it asked me to type in the city I wanted to visit – the street, house number and postcode.

So far it was impressive, but not worth anywhere near what I'd paid for it. I scrolled to a third screen and it was quite confusing to look at. In the top left hand corner it said, *Date* and *Time*. In the top right hand corner was *Time* and *Place*. In the bottom left hand corner was *Space-Time Coordinates Before*, and in the bottom right hand corner was *Space-Time Location After*. Plus and minus signs were placed in the middle of the screen above four digital dials that had Einstein's famous $E=MC2$ equation below them, which I thought was strange. What did his equation have to do with the workings of a Sat-Nav? Well, at this point I was so tired that I couldn't be bothered to investigate further, so I turned the mechanism off and went up to bed for an early night. And my last thought before falling asleep was – I *wish* I could go back in time, stop my wife being murdered and have my life back as it was.

Chapter 3

Early the next morning I called in at my office to cancel my appointments for the next two weeks. I had decided to take a break and was going to Sterling in Scotland. I needed a complete break away from everybody and everything, but mainly work. Wrapping up a couple of small matters that needed my immediate attention, I told the office staff and part-time clerks doing the research for my case-load where they could reach me if something urgent came up that needed my input – but other than that, not to try and get in touch. I had to get away. Be alone!

***

WHEN I ARRIVED IN STERLING it was cold, grey and miserable, but it felt good just to be *alone*. Driving through the heavy traffic it had taken the best part of seven hours to reach the jagged peaks of Scotland, which cut into a sky masked with clouds and trailers of mist. Mountains glistened through a steady downpour, but the grass and heather smelt so good to me. However, I was staggered by the long drive and felt like a corpse awaiting life. *I'll sleep soundly tonight,* I thought.

I was staying in a log cabin, by a little known lake I'd discovered some years earlier quite by chance. It isn't on any map that I know of, because it's so remote, and the cabin is very basic and no *Waldorf Hotel* with modern conveniences such as plush carpets or televisions, but that's exactly why I go there – for the solitude. It took me just five minutes to unpack as I'd brought very little with me other than clothes and food. Oh, and a few bottles of my favourite scotch, my mobile and new Sat-Nav, which was still in its case. I didn't need it to get to the cabin because I knew the roads like the back of my hand.

I looked at my watch. 4:00 pm. Time to relax and have a

drink. I poured myself a scotch and water and sat down on the hard couch. Taking out the Sun newspaper I'd brought with me, I opened it and scanned the columns, frowning. There had been twenty teenage stabbings reported in London in one month, and God knows how many *unreported.* I wondered how people could kill each other so casually and turned to the sports section. It covered the week's football matches and it was football... football... football. Not for me thank you! I'm interested in boxing and ice hockey and that's it – the 'Chicago Blackhawks' being my favourite hockey team.

Sipping at my scotch, I threw the newspaper to one side, ruminating thoughtfully. I was getting better. *I was.* I knew I was. I didn't need the doctors any more, I was doing it myself, one step at a time, and had left my many problems behind me at home. The open spaces and fresh air would benefit me greatly. It had in the past. Now there were no cars, trains, airplanes, material possessions or creature comforts – well, not many. I had left most of the modern things behind me and was even sleeping on a hard pallet bed, but didn't mind. Nor did I mind the wind and rain. I wanted to get back to nature because this is who I am.

I decided that I would go fishing for the first week of my vacation and camping for the following week, not that my plans ever work out the way they're supposed to. *I'll probably end up in Oz,* I thought, *following the yellow brick road with the tin man, lion and scarecrow, chased by the munchkins and stalked by the wicked witch of the west.* I wondered what it would be like. Certainly more exciting than my life had been up to date without my beloved Jane. *Stop it. Stop it, this is doing no good!* I shook my head.

My gaze wandered over to the small leather case of the very expensive and exclusive, one-of-a-kind, collectors-item, Sat-

Nav. I stood, walked across the room and picked it up. Opening the case I stared at the glittering, metallic machine. It was scarcely larger than a calculator and very delicately made, like an expensive Swiss watch. I switched it on and there seemed to be a breath of wind in the cabin and the lights dimmed. Automatically it scrolled to the third screen, showing Einstein's equation: $E=MC^2$. Then to my amazement, it asked in a whisper, "Into the future or back to the past?"

I stooped to look down at the screen incredulously.

"Do you desire the near future or distant past, Time Traveller?" it asked again.

My eyes grew larger, brighter, but I felt the colour drain from my cheeks. "This is a joke, right?" I said to myself aloud.

"I cannot calculate your comments, Time Traveller," said the machine, "only Length, Breadth, Width and Duration. I know nothing of *joke*, it does not compute. Only instantaneous existence will compute – recalculating..."

"I must be dreaming," I said, my mind racing.

"Cannot compute *dreaming* – recalculating..."

My glance flickered over the machine's shiny face with a certain dull approval and then around the room. *If I'm not dreaming this is some sort of trick and there must be a microphone and video camera hidden in here somewhere,* I thought. Curiously, I walked over to the mirror, lifting it slightly. There was nothing behind it except for the hard wooden wall. I searched the couch, curtains and throws for microphones, but there was nothing. I even lifted the hearthrug, which was stupid of me. Then, for a minute perhaps, I stood ruminating thoughtfully again, trying to figure it out.

Any spectator watching me will be staring at my flushed, animated face, I thought. *It's quite a good practical joke – almost believable.* Perplexed by it, I was. There was a dull whine and a click from the machine and it began to buzz oddly. Then the machine asked, "Space Time Coordinates or Favourite Time and Place, Time Traveller? Enter now..."

I scanned the machine's liquid crystal face as it gave me orders.

"Verbal commands only for Favourite Time and Place," it said, actually sounding quite irritated by my lack of action in carrying out its commands. The artificial voice quavered, resonating deeply and it even sighed at my delay.

"Don't understand you," I told the machine, and it actually seemed to become pensive, its gears and mechanisms clicking away as if in real thought.

"There are four dimensions in your world. They are the Space-Time Continuum. Three are the planes of Space and the fourth is *Time* and grossly overlooked as a dimension. It is, however, a dimension nevertheless, and if its course is charted it can be travelled. For this reason, there is no difference between the Fourth Dimension and the three dimensions of Space," the machine enlightened. Its steady confident voice seemed to be gloating at my lack of knowledge on the subject. "Time is lazy," it continued, "but dynamic. It's honeycombed with capsules of captured time and has its own code. It is also a billion times thinner than a human hair, but strong enough to bind the three dimensions of Space together. Time *is* stable, but shifts constantly, which is why I am a ground-breaking machine. I *can* follow those shifts!"

Incredibly, I began to believe what was happening and the possibilities seemed literally endless. I had gained the machine by default when a mysterious catalogue addressed to someone else had arrived at my door, and I had paid an exorbitant price over the phone with my credit card for something that usually costs less than two hundred pounds, so it certainly seemed like fate had a hand in it somehow.

There I was, grieving for my lost love – my wife – and I

somehow manage to get my hands on a Time Machine. *If it's the genuine article, I can go back in time and change what has happened,* I thought. *Jane won't be murdered. I can stop it.* But then, every time-travelling film I've ever seen has always maintained that you can't change the past, because it will alter the future and cause a time paradox. However, what if I go back in time to before the killing, kidnap the murderer and take him to the distant future, to earth's last day ever, and dump his ass there. He couldn't kill my wife then. How could he? And it couldn't change anything, because time would be at an end for planet earth.

I felt almost cheerful for the first time in years and yet I still found this all too surreal, because it seemed like some sleight-of-hand-trick or other – something a conjurer would dream up. I smiled to myself faintly. "This has got to be humbug, an extravagant theory concocted by a hoaxer. It can't be true. It just can't be!"

I turned the machine off, walked slowly out of the room in my slippers and shuffled down the long passage towards the bedroom, placing it on my bedside table. I put my hands deep into my trouser pockets, shuffling back to the living area where I sat down. I've always been a doubter, a sceptic, but what if by pure chance it is a *Time Machine.* The possibilities were staggering. Even on a lighter note, I could simply invest my life's savings and leave it to accumulate at a high rate of interest, and then rush on ahead into the future to reap what I had sown years earlier. That isn't changing the future. It's simply manipulating the past and harmless with no consequences. Or so I thought.

On an even lighter note, I could go back in time and see myself being born. That would be worth seeing. However, again it was a wild extravagant theory, even though a plausible one. I puzzled matters through. *If I could go back in time, would I be like a ghost if I didn't want to show myself?*

Or would my form be solid and as vulnerable as I am now? I just couldn't stop deliberating on the matter, and I'll be honest and tell you the truth, it excited me beyond all imagination.

But, I'm a clever lawyer and only believe in hard facts that stand up in the cold light of day, and don't disappear under the ever-watchful eye of another's stern gaze. Even if I saw God, I would still have to touch him, smell him and hear him before I would believe. And however plausible the machine might seem, it might somehow disappear right before my eyes – as had the photograph and listing in the catalogue. Therefore, if this is all an extravagant, elaborate joke, played on me by one of my friends to distract me from a world of pain, it's of epic proportions.

I stood up, paced across the room and poured myself a scotch and water. *I need to know if the machine works or not,* I thought, *I won't sleep until I know one way or the other. I can't wait for common sense to come tomorrow morning. I want to know now!* I needed to see the machine again, to look at its parts of brass, nickel and ivory. It was a beautifully crafted thing of intricate design. I shuffled back down the long, draughty passageway to the bedroom, picked up the machine from my dresser top and turned it on. Once again there was a breath of fresh air and the lights dimmed as it scrolled to the third screen and asked, "Favourite Time and Place? Input verbally!"

If indeed the machine did work, I didn't want to go too far into the past or future, just in case I couldn't get back. So I thought I'd play it safe. "I want to go back to yesterday, at precisely 3:45 pm, here in Sterling, Scotland, to this cabin I'm staying in by this lake," I ordered as explicitly as I could.

Instantly, my mind seemed to reel in a kind of fog and I felt the weirdest sensation – one of weightlessness, of flying, but looking about me it seemed as if nothing had happened. Then, I saw myself walk into the room with my bags. I drew a deep breath, watching, gritting my teeth as everything flickered hazily and went dark. Suddenly a strange confusion descended upon me, but it was excessively pleasant. *The machine works! It really does work!* I thought, *I'm here watching myself arrive and unpack, how cool is that!* It was simply unbelievable!

I looked at the clock on the mantelpiece. It was precisely 3:45 pm, the exact time I had arrived at the cabin. I drew a deeper breath and everything went hazy and dark again as I watched. I was confused. I was here both times – now and then – so why couldn't my past-self see my future time travelling self? And the only smart answer that I could come up with was that because I was time-travelling, I was moving too fast through the same space. *That's the time paradox*, I thought with an air of impartiality. *My past self can't see me any more than I can see the spokes of a spinning wheel, or a bullet fired from a gun, if it's moving a thousand times faster than normal speed. I'll get through a day in a minute, while someone who is not time travelling will get through a minute in a minute.*

I watched myself traverse the cabin, seeming to shoot from room to room like a rocket, unpacking my odds, ends and belongings, and then make a drink, take a bath, dress and finally retire to my bed for the night, all in little more than the blink of an eye. However, I didn't dare order the machine to slow down or stop, for fear of colliding with myself. I didn't know what would happen if I did. Would *I* cease to exist if I met my past self?

Time Travel really does exist, I thought, *and it's a peculiar sensation. The constant bucking and buffeting feeling is of a helpless headlong motion, which gives the impression that a great crash is coming.*

Finally, my curiosity satisfied, I ordered the machine to take me back to the present day. And in a great blur of blinding coloured light with huge noises filling my ears, and a strange numbness in my mind, it did. I switched the machine off, staring at it in amazement. I had been propelled through time with great velocity like a vapour through thin air, ghostlike and unnoticed by my past self. I had done something that as far as I knew had never – in all of history – ever been done before. I *had* time-travelled and shot through the Fourth Dimension with the speed of a bullet, and the only risk was that I should somehow come to a jarring halt inside of something solid, smashing me to pieces, tearing every particle of my fragile being apart in one great chain-reaction of an explosion. I supposed that it could have far-reaching effects upon the four dimensions, let alone me. However, I had to accept that as an unavoidable risk.

On the plus side, it now seemed plausible that I could not only go anywhere, but I could also visit any time period – past or future – before returning to my comfortable existence in the present. And my only fear was of the *Unknown*. I decided there and then to keep an explicit journal of my exploits, the first part of which was to make a list of times and places to visit, of famous people who have influenced society universally with great ideas, great inventions and exercised strong and lasting influences on subsequent generations – people with remarkable reputations like the prophets who anticipated flying machines, tanks and the inevitable nuclear bomb.

Now, I could go *anywhere*, skipping through the centuries at will almost, to prove theories or dispel myths. Who really shot John F Kennedy? Did Marilyn Monroe commit suicide? There may even be evidence locked away somewhere that the 'Roswell Alien Incident' really happened in the 1940's. I could probably go back in time and prove whether Jesus ever existed, and if so, whether he was really a miracle worker or a marvelous magician. Did he really do the impossible and make a blind man see, turn water into wine, feed five thousand people with two fish and five loaves? Or were they merely mass hypnotic illusions?

Maybe I'll sweep back into the past, where huge grotesque dinosaurs roam in the Jurassic period, or sweep forward billions of years to watch the end of our world as the sun's fuel finally burns out and it grows into a red giant, eventually engulfing the whole solar system, killing us all. I began to realise that I could watch and be untouched, simply because the laws of physics say so. Now, someone could finally go back in time and answer the riddles of the ages. *Me!*

Chapter 4

I somehow had to be calm and patient and not go too far, too fast. I had to grow with the machine, expand my knowledge of its working and find out if it had limitations that might somehow cause me great harm or, even worse – *kill me*. I needed to know a lot more about it before I could venture into the distant past or the far-flung future.

It was now that I decided to experiment with the past, rather than the future, conducting a few intricate experiments to see whether I could influence my own personal history, and one event in particular that had happened in my boxing career – the knock-out that had finished it. Could I have won the fight that night if I'd had the foresight to see the uppercut coming? Maybe now I could go back in time to that all-important fateful night, armed with the knowledge of what was to happen, and exactly when my opponent would fire that devastating shot that would lift me from the canvas, almost taking my bloody head off. But could I actually change what had happened that night? Forewarned is forearmed they say, but I still doubted whether I could change anything. I went to bed and dreamt that I *could*.

***

EARLY THE NEXT MORNING, after a breakfast of bacon, eggs and tomatoes and the mandatory cup of coffee, I made notes of the knock-out night in question, when I ended up flat on my back, out cold – and for the count. I wrote down the time, place and other relevant details. It was Bethnal Green at 7:45pm, on the night of 27th September. I remember it so well because it was my birthday. I was twenty years old that day and the year was 1982.

I went to the bedroom and picked up the Time Machine from my dresser, unlocking the leather case, once again staring at it with incredulity like a man recovering from a stupor. I switched it on and the familiar voice asked, "Space Time Coordinates?"

I had no idea what *Space Time Coordinates* were, so I relayed to the machine the information I had written down.

"*Calculating,*" it said flatly.

"Great," said I, smiling like a Cheshire Cat. Suddenly there was the usual breath of wind, the lights flickered and the room became indistinct as my reflection in the mirror became hazy, g*hostlike,* flickering in and out of sight. Everything was silent for a moment as my reflection vanished completely from the mirror. Then there was a loud click, a dull drone and my mind reeled from the mad feeling of falling through time.

Once again it was a feeling of rushing headlong towards some great collision with an immovable object. It made me feel nauseous – violently sick in the pit of my stomach. *Will I be smashed to pieces this time?* After a short interval of feeling ghastly, everything went black and I passed out. I was glad because it stopped that awful, sickly, falling feeling.

Now there was a flash of blinding light and a great confusion of noise around me. My eyes opened. I'd done it. I was there, back in time.

"Stay down kid, it's all over!" That's all I could hear, besides the referee counting slowly. My life, career and dreams ebbed away with those few haunting words. I shook my head in disbelief. I shook it again, trying to regain my senses. *Was this the way it was supposed to end? Didn't I have a say in the matter?*

Again the words, "Stay down kid," echoed around me from somewhere outside the ring. It was my trainer's voice, Harry South, clear as day. But I couldn't think straight. My mind was completely detached from my body. Again I shook my head, blood dripping from the cuts above my eyes and I crawled towards my corner out of pure instinct, because I couldn't see a damn thing.

Suddenly my vision cleared and I saw Harry's lined face, tortured and twisted as if caught in a vice. He was screaming like a maniac, "Stay down kid, he'll kill you! You can't win!"

Bloodied and battered, I crawled for what seemed an eternity. Finally reaching my corner, I turned and looked up to see my opponent, Jess Cooper, laughing at me with a mean menacing look on his face.

"Told you I'd whip your over-confident ass! The smart money was always on me!" he announced for all to hear.

The words rang louder in my ears than the referee counting the seconds, and stung much more than my cuts and bruises ever would. *I'm the better fighter,* I thought. *So why am I on the canvas and not him?* And the only reason I could think of, was that someone had drugged the water in my corner, because it had such a strange bitter taste. I had started going light-headed from the very first bell, and even though I'd fought like a lion and had him down on the canvas three times from great head and body shots, it was me who had been lying spread-eagled on the canvas moments earlier.

Again I could hear Harry screaming, *"Stay down you idiot, he'll kill your ass!"* I pulled myself up onto the top rope and turned to see Jess still smiling his unique malicious smile, his red gum-shield almost popping out of the corner of his mouth. He was relishing the moment, enjoying every second of his night's work, beckoning for me to get up and fight some more so that he could punish me further. And I realised that I had absolutely nothing left to give.

The crowd was on their feet, frenzied and hysterical, most of them shouting my name, telling me to get up and fight. A throng of Cooper's ardent fans called me a *bum* and gave advice like "throw in the towel" and "stay down or die". It seemed like good advice.

I looked up at the clear glass auditorium fanlight and it was raining heavily outside. But then, it had been raining heavily on the inside, mostly punches on me. Ask me tomorrow and I'll swear I was hit by thunder and lightning in the ring too. I think I even found God in there. Because when Cooper was hitting me with everything in his well-honed armoury, someone's voice kept telling me to get up – and a power greater than me kept on getting me up.

It's funny when you're out there alone in the centre of the ring, whether you're on your feet or your back is to the canvas, you seem to hear every single voice in the room, and I kept hearing one in particular tonight saying, "Get up, ya bum, he ain't laid a glove on ya yet!" And I kept thinking: *Well then someone had better keep an eye on the ref, 'cause somebody sure as hell is hitting me.*

I looked back down from the fanlight, instantly recognising my daughter's face. Olivia was at the back of the auditorium with her mum and they were both in tears, shouting, "We love you!" at the top of their voices. And in that single moment, something charged me with a power beyond all reason. Was it the *Time Traveller* within me? It was as if someone had literally plugged me into the mains and switched me on, and my only thought was that I couldn't let them see me fail. Not again!

I had moulded myself on great roll-models like Mohammad Ali, George Foreman and Sugar Ray Leonard, none of whom gave up in the ring until the last bell. Yes, you could knock them down, but they always got back up, and in most cases went on to win. Usually in the most unusual circumstances and always in the most dramatic way. Many a contest has been won by the underdog who's been written off at the start of the fight – but it only takes one hard, lucky punch to change everything around.

I can still win. I know what he's going to do and when he's going to do it. And there are still two rounds to go. I have to dig deep and think positive. Wait for the right moment. It's not every day you get a second chance, I thought, shaking my head.

I wiped the blood from my eyes, trying to clear my vision, and I stared across the auditorium at my wife and daughter. They were still sobbing buckets of tears. *I can't leave it here, not now. I might as well just die in the ring. Because if I lose with Time on my side, what's the point.*

My mind drifted back to a book I once read, about a man who ate an airplane. Its title was: "The Man Who Ate the 747". He did it to prove his love for a woman, who incidentally didn't love him back, and it was supposedly a true story, reported at the time by an official working for The Guinness Book of Records. And I thought, *if someone can somehow grind a whole airplane to pieces, add it to their food and eat it over a period of months or years for the love of a woman, then I'm damn sure I can dredge up the strength to win this Goddamn fight.*

Seconds ticked away. The bell rang to end the tenth round. Harry jumped into the ring and sat me on my stool, screaming for me to let him throw in the towel. I shook my head, not having the strength to speak. He screamed at me again and I shook my head again. Jim Phelps, my cut man, jumped into the ring too and began working on my eyes with extraordinary speed. Harry, still screaming, wafted me with his towel. "Breathe! Get some air into those lungs kid!" Then ironically he said what I'd just been thinking. "If you're gonna do this, don't leave it out there – die in the ring!"

It was a really weird sensation reliving the past. I knew everything Harry was going to say to me and how he would say it. I knew Jim would staunch the blood from my cuts to allow me to continue, and I also knew the bombs that were going to hit me. And for that reason, all I had to do was get the timing right. Nodding, I tried to smile but the cuts in my mouth wouldn't let me and I kept my gum-shield in, staying away from the water, drugged or not.

"Get some air! Get some air!" Harry shouted, furiously massaging my arms and legs. Dipping his sponge into a bucket of water, he wiped the blood from my face while Jim frantically worked on my cuts with the adrenaline cream and swabs. I shook my head again and my mind began to clear.

"Stay on the cuts!" Harry shouted.

Jim worked furiously. "How do you feel?"

"Worse than I look probably," I answered.

"You… you sure you can do this, kid?" Harry asked in a whisper, smiling sympathetically, but looking horror struck.

I nodded, gasping for air, trying to raise a smile. "Don't have a choice, do I? Got to rise to the occasion!"

Harry rubbed and massaged my legs and arms once more. Jim finalised my cuts. Both stared at me with a steely gaze. Then the bell rang for the eleventh round to begin. "Good luck kid!" they said in unison, climbing out through the ropes. "Don't leave it out there! Resolve the situation and kill the bum!" That was Harry's final advice.

I got off my stool, heading for the centre of the ring and began to jab, bob and weave. He came at me like a train. I knew he would. He hooked to my ribs and I covered up with my elbows. He hooked to my head and I covered up with my gloves. I thundered an uppercut into his chin and his face twisted and distorted as if he'd been hit by a truck, but he smiled at me coldly, putting his hands up in the air and the crowd cheered. *Are they cheering him or me,* I thought?

I got up onto my toes, dancing around the ring as I'd seen the greats do in their time, and I banged away at the body, trying to make his head fall. I couldn't believe how well I was doing. It was almost too good to be true. His face was beginning to redden, blister and swell and one eye looked like it had a raw potato stuffed under the skin.

He snarled at me. "You're dead meat!" He spat his gum-shield in my face. I took the initiative and jabbed while his mouth was unprotected, knocking out a tooth and he smiled and spat that in my face too. *I'm gonna have to kill him to win*, I thought.

Harry was screaming all kinds of instructions from outside the ropes and was ducking and diving more than I was. "Keep working! Keep working! Use those combinations!"

Jess and I were toe to toe now, banging away at each other furiously. I hooked him. He counter-punched and jabbed me. We clinched, our eyes fixed on each other. Then he hit me with a low blow without the referee noticing and the closer it got to the end of the round, the better I thought I was doing. It was the fight of my life, against my toughest opponent.

With ten seconds left to go in the round I back pedalled, taking a breather, and it was the biggest mistake of my whole career – but one that I now knew how to rectify. I have never been a good defensive fighter, and am only good going forward, so when he caught me completely off guard and off balance with a devastating uppercut that made my feet leave the canvas – the lights went *out*.

However, from somewhere past my subconscious, I heard the referee start the count and my eyes popped wide open again. I shook my head. I shook it again. And because of my inner time-travelling self it felt like I was floating somewhere overhead, looking down on the scene.

I was flat on my back, down and almost out and could hear Harry and Jim screaming. "Oh my God! Oh – my – good God! There's no way he'll get up from that!"

And all I could think about and remember was how my time travelling had begun a few days earlier, and whether I could really change the outcome. Well, I went back to that fateful night five times. Yes, it took *five* attempts to get the timing right and miss that devastating uppercut that Jess would throw at me, but I finally got it right and went on to win in the last round with my own bombshell of an uppercut, changing the past and my boxing career. But could I stop my wife's murder? Was that possible?

Chapter 5
STIRLING. SCOTLAND. PRESENT DAY.

I leapt back to the present day a happy man. I had always wanted to be a fighter – a real contender. It's what I've always done best.

Fighters come from everywhere, all lifestyles, and each has a different story to tell. My father was a heroic man, a boxer too, but he was also a lieutenant in the navy, inserted in an undisclosed site outside of Korea in the 1950's. He was in harm's way most of the time, and as a small child I just wanted him home safe. It was heart-warming when he did come home too. The first thing we did was to give him a big hug and say we were glad to see him, glad he was home safe and in one piece. The lost finger or toe, black eye or broken nose didn't seem to matter too much, because we were just glad to see him alive. Some of his best friends were killed in one way or another – a knife, hand-grenade or bomb. So the look on our faces as he walked back through the door after the war ended must have been phenomenal. He's dead now and I still miss him. He died of a heart attack, aged fifty-eight.

Looking back on my own boxing career my abilities seemed unique at the time, but the same story is worldwide. It's about love, dignity and courage. We're men, fathers, sons and brothers with one common goal – to be the best of the best. Now when I look at my scrapbook, my boxing career remains unblemished. I retired undefeated, just because I had time on my side for once in my life, thanks to a machine the size of a calculator.

So, I began to develop new ideas about time-travelling. It seemed that I could go back into the past and relive events in my body, or go back and watch certain events unfold as an unnoticed spectre. A *ghostly* spectator if you like. On the one hand, I could simply watch what others did in the past, while on the other hand I could actually participate. *Would this be the same for the future,* I pondered? I needed to test my theories a little more before venturing too far into the future or the past. However, I began to feel like a *god,* omnipotent, almighty and all-powerful! Finally, my life seemed to be emerging from the dreadful shadows of grief, and the best thing was that even though I had changed my boxing career, I hadn't altered anything else – or so it seemed. I hadn't caused a "Time Paradox" with my crude intervention. I hadn't even caused a ripple in the Fourth Dimension.

It seemed a peculiar thing, wandering through time – a motion like no other. There was an overwhelming feeling of speed, but at the same time it was like trying to pull free of a thick gelatinous mass that was holding me prisoner. Going backwards in time made my eyes bulge, lungs burn and limbs ache. I supposed the feelings would be much the same roaming forward in time, or possibly worse as I entered the Unknown. I wondered if God had *fixed* the future for all time. Or could I change it, as I had the past?

In the future, will creatures from another world invade the earth? And if so, will we overcome them? Or will it once again be populated by incredible creatures, half human and half animal as in the distant past. Will we still be capable of thought and speech? Or will it be combined one day as our brainpower grows? These are just a few of the questions I needed answering and there are literally thousands more.

Now I have in my possession a tool like no other, a magic lamp almost, to grant my every wish from time to time, but I don't mind telling you all that I became pensive about the matter of *Time* and *Time Travel,* as it's only natural for a rational man to question something that seems irrational. At least I think so. People who spout mystic words constantly do not necessarily know the meaning of them, if indeed they have a meaning. Pretenders and charlatans spring to mind, of which there have been many in any given field over the centuries, from the psychic and paranormal to the everyday man in the street. Well, I need concrete proof before I believe anything, and now I had that proof. Time travel is possible, but to what degree? To what end?

I decided that my wife's murder was the most important event of my whole life. Nothing else could compare to it. Everything else paled in significance and like my children, I was devastated by that single act, because it had been cold, calculated and brutal. Jane had her throat slit in such a way that it had nearly decapitated her, but even worse was the fact that she had to endure rape and torture before the final act, and it had filtered so deep into my subconscious that dreadful nightmares visited me every single night.

Not only did I want to go back in time to try to stop it. I had to! It was a compulsion beyond all others. I had loved her with a passion, beyond all reason, and still do. My children do too. I rationalised that if I could go back in time and change my boxing career, then the same would apply to my wife's murder, and it wouldn't alter the lives of others. However, even to this day I'm not sure whether I'm right or wrong, because I've propelled myself back to that awful night at least one hundred times, only to watch my wife die over and over again without being able to stop it. In this one instance, I haven't been able to change what has already happened – and I can't figure out *why?*

I had done it so successfully once before, so I'll never give up trying, but I need to know a lot more about the three dimensions of Space and the geometry of the Fourth Dimension first. For instance, I have already learned that as the earth rotates and moves around the sun, time does not occupy the same space, which is why clocks are set differently all over the world, and there *is* a simple calculation which computes the differences – although I'll be damned if I can remember what it is.

I decided to investigate further. And so, the next few days were a blur of activity, besides being exhausting, although I neither went camping nor fishing. Instead, I instructed my Time Machine to visit the past, and to be specific, the "Piper Alpha Oil Platform Disaster" in the North Sea, east off Aberdeen, mid-afternoon on July 6th 1988. I leapt back in my ghostly form so that I would be protected from harm, and I watched it explode and erupt into a giant fireball, killing nearly everyone on board.

I leapt back further. But only two years, to the "Chernobyl Nuclear Reactor Disaster", on April 26th of 1986, again in mid-afternoon in the Ukraine, in the U.S.S.R., and was horrified that civilian firemen were sent into the reactor to clean it up without protective clothing after the explosion. Subsequently, they all died of radiation poisoning.

I stayed in the same year and watched the Challenger Space Shuttle blow up on January 10th – mid-morning at Cape Canaveral in the U.S.A. All on board were killed instantly as the shuttle blew into thousands of pieces, because a tiny part called an *O Ring* failed inside the booster rocket.

I roamed further back in time, to October 20th of 1966 and the "Abervan Mud Slide Disaster", in Wales, near Merthyr Tydfil, to watch a mountain of mud slurry sweep over a primary school, crushing it, killing many children. It was horrific. Heart rending. But I had to find out *what*, if anything could have been done to stop these disasters from happening.

I went even further back to watch the Hindenburg airship explode on May 6th in 1937, late afternoon in New Jersey at Lakehurst. I watched the Titanic sink on April 15th in 1912, after midnight in the North Atlantic, off Newfoundland.

I went further and further back, to the "Great Fire of London", watching the fire start on Pudding Lane and saw the city burn to the ground. It was terrifying to watch, to say the least.

Then, I went to see Sir Francis Drake play bowls on the bowling greens of Dover, before setting sail to meet the Spanish Armada. I watched in awed silence. He beat them exactly as was recorded in history, by bouncing his cannonballs off the surface of the sea to gain extra length and power, in the same way a flat stone can be skipped across the surface of a lake.

As I plunged through time, I experienced every emotion from sadness to joy. The sadness for the many lives lost. The joy mostly from the experience of navigating through the ages. And in my dealing with the *Time Machine,* I discovered certain valuable information quite by accident, and one cannot but choose to wonder whether I'll keep on discovering more and more as time slips by.

For instance, I discovered quite by chance that there was a removable micro-chip on the back of the machine, and then I discovered its specific use. If I removed the micro-chip, but kept it about my person and we were somehow separated in time, the machine and I, it would seek me out. It was a kind of homing beacon. *Ingenious and invaluable,* I thought.

It also came to me quite by chance that the machine had a kind of a key on the side. Its use was also very ingenious. If something went disastrously wrong while I was time travelling, I could remove the key. It would then undo anything that I might have done to cause the destructive "Time Paradox" scenario. It certainly seemed like I'd gotten my monies worth now, when the five thousand pounds disappeared from my bank account along with the mysterious photograph and catalogue listing, because now there were so many choices to make in my life.

After Jane's death I felt like a dull stone, whereas now I feel like a polished diamond. How could anyone else even imagine the power of my small machine, and it was proving invaluable to me personally, helping me see things from a totally different perspective, time and again.

I never went back to my job at the Law Practice, and a whole year passed in the blink of an eye as I wandered down the centuries, watching and collating evidence that time travel really does exist, and I did it without intruding at all. I used my spectral self, more than my physical self to digitally video actual events as proof of my ageless globe-trotting around Time.

However, I did it for *me* more than anyone else, because I still needed a distraction in my sad life, and as much as I was enjoying time travel, I couldn't help but feel that it would have been a million times better with Jane by my side. Anyway, I decided to restrict my time-travelling to the daytime when my kids were at school, and made sure I was always home on time to pick them back up. I would travel through a whole century, watching it change to the next century, and be back in my own time and hardly an hour would have passed. I observed major land and sea battles from the beginning of time that lasted days, weeks or months and it took mere minutes. I did go back and visit with Jesus too, and the feeding of the five thousand was as I suspected – a case of *Chinese Whispers*. He did however, feed five hundred people with two massive tuna fish weighing five hundred pounds or more each, and five loaves of bread that were so big they would be in the Guinness Book of Records if someone baked them like that today.

I also visited the Walls of Jericho out of curiosity, at the time the Bible says they were crumbled by the blowing of a thousand horns, and as much as I would love to believe in miracles, it didn't quite happen that way. There was a terrific earthquake at the exact moment the soldiers in question were blowing their horns. The walls did crumble nevertheless.

I say for my own part, that I have learned there is always a glimmer of truth somewhere in the dark recesses of the past, and on my many adventures, I began to wonder whether I should ever return to my own time – but then I thought of my children. How could I even think of leaving them behind, for they *are* the best part of me, and I would have loved to have more children if the unthinkable hadn't happened, cutting Jane's life short by at least two score years.

All the while, I distracted myself by visiting the abyss of the Cretaceous Sea, and then the Jurassic period on land, noted for its grotesque saurian brutes. I observed unnoticed, Plesiosaurs, which hunted the vast Oolitic coral reefs in the Triassic Age too. All were unbelievably amazing experiences. Truly beyond belief. But then, what could any man say when he'd had such experiences as these, for it seemed that history was teaching me living lessons time and time again.

But my most recent lesson to date, way back in prehistory, was sixty five million years ago. I watched the death of the dinosaurs as a rock the size of Mount Everest came hurtling in from space at seven miles per second, and blasted millions of tons of earth up into the atmosphere, blotting out the sun for years. I watched the blast in great detail, over and over again in replay – another feature of my Time Machine. I was hypnotized with shock and awe. The blast impact was hotter than the surface of the sun, and anything within a thousand miles radius was instantly incinerated. Vapourised! It was hell on earth, and because it crashed into the sea at the Yucatan Peninsula, near Mexico, the shock-wave also created a giant tsunami with waves up to three or four hundred feet high, moving at an average speed of 400 miles per hour, destroying and killing everything in its wake. Half the planet was a fireball. Half was flooded.

The final nail in the coffin for the dinosaurs, and some of the mammals roaming the earth, was that the asteroid couldn't possibly have hit a worse place on the planet. It was rich with all the elements needed to cause such a vast disaster and created deadly global chaos. Not only did the food chain collapse and the animals starve because of acid rain, but the whole world was eventually choked for hundreds of years by sulphur and carbon dioxide, which blotted out the sun.

After a hundred and sixty million years the dinosaurs' rule had finally come to a catastrophic end, but some mammals survived. We did, our descendants, because we became generalists – omnivores that would eat literally anything. So life on earth began again and *I* saw it all happen!

The *Time Machine* instructed me in so many things. However, what it wasn't teaching me was how I could change the past, present or future for the better good. I knew I could. I'd done it before. So why couldn't I do it again?

I had, at first, thought time travel impossible like most rational beings, but I had been proved wrong by something with the computing power of a battery operated calculator, nothing more. Had this small machine come from the future? Was it sent back to my time in some sort of bizarre experiment to see what would happen? Indeed, there seemed to be no rational explanation that answered my questions.

And so, night after night I slept upon the problem, but with the rising of the morning sun I was no wiser. Until one fine day when the answer hit me like a brick on the head. When I went back in time to change my boxing career, I *must* have altered something else. *I must have!* It's got to be why I can't change things now.

God in his infinite wisdom gave us all *Free Will*, but not free reign over the universe. Again I was struck as by a thunderbolt. Did Einstein's equation E= MC2 on the third screen have anything to do with shaping or altering time. Had the solution been staring me in the face the whole time? Is man's *Free Will* the deciding factor in the outcome of an event, because we're fallible and make mistakes? A ship designed not to sink could still sink with a captain at the helm who ignores sound advice, just as an airplane designed to fly will crash because of human error. That has to be the answer. To change my wife's past, so that she lives, I had to know what the murderer was thinking and doing just prior to the murder and then everything will be fine. I had to *stop* him, instead of trying to *save* her!

At this time, close friends began to suggest that I was becoming indifferent and lazy because I was ignoring my law career, which I had ditched without a second thought. I began getting depressed again because I couldn't prove my critics wrong. The Time Machine, however, stopped me worrying. I was moving on to greener pastures and would prove them wrong. "Forget the ungrateful back-stabbers," I told myself, "they're not even worth the trouble." *What did they know anyway?*

I decided to go back in time to the 25th of July, 2008, one day before my wife's murder, to a bar called Fat Jack's on the Old Kent Road in London, to start my investigation of the events surrounding her death. After her murder, I had read in the London Times that there had been some kind of a disturbance there the day before. I set the machine and pressed the necessary buttons. In a blinding flash I was sitting in Fat Jack's in my physical form, watching events unfold.

It was humid inside the bar and the heat of the summer day

seemed to be getting hotter by the second. I felt a trickle of sweat drip between my shoulder blades and dabbed my forehead. Just then, two mean looking men came walking in with a cocky swagger. One was an impossibly big man, six feet eight or so, and as wide as a bear. The other was small and stocky with a long thin scar running the length of his cheek. They sat down on the bar stools, ordered drinks in a bullying voice and began laughing and joking loudly, irritating the other customers for over an hour. Finally the barman asked them to shut up and be quiet, or leave.

The big man, answering to the name of Terry Doonan stared hard at the barman, his gaze unblinking. "I want another drink! And I want it now!" he said in the same bullying voice.

I watched the barman shake his head. "You've had enough already."

Terry turned his head, watching his friend taking a swallow of scotch. "How's things at home, these days?" he inquired.

Frankie smacked his lips deliberately, burping richly.

I began to listen carefully to their conversation, watching the events of the day unfold. There was a drink on my table that someone had left, so I picked it up and sipped at the cheap rum. It tasted quite pleasant.

Finally, Frankie answered. "Things were okay until my fuckin' dog almost bit my hand off. I was in hospital three days. But when I got out I cornered the mutt, stuck a gun in its mouth and *BAM!* Blew its fuckin' skull all over the place..."

Terry stared hard at Frankie. "I loved that dog," he protested. Sighing he sat back, plucking a hand rolled cigarette from his shirt pocket, and then he produced a paper of matches in his other hand and tore one off, running it across the friction strip, lighting the cigarette, inhaling slowly, thoughtfully. "I *did* love that dog."

"I did too," said Frankie, genuinely saddened, "but you

should never bite the hand that feeds you, particularly when your owner's got a gun in the other fuckin' hand. Now I've got a finger missing and thirty stitches." He took a long swallow of his scotch, smacking his lips, burping loudly in his friend's face.

"Thanks! I could almost taste that!" said Terry, looking as hard as nails. "Think yourself lucky I don't slap your arrogant face!"

I kept watching. Eavesdropping all the while. Frankie stared at Terry and grinned. "You're welcome..."

"What's so fuckin' amusin'?" asked Terry, shooting his friend a dark look.

"Just thinkin', gonna be a long old day, eh? But by tonight I'll be ten thousand pounds richer, and lyin' in my nice warm bed, watchin' telly with my old lady. What will you be doin'?"

"I'll be doin' your old lady if you don't make it back tonight," said Terry with a wry smile. He pushed a black cloth bag across the table. "That's for you. You sure you're up for this?"

I watched Frankie open the bag. There was a 9mm Beretta and two spare clips of ammo in it. I was shocked. Horrified.

"Sure," he nodded. "Lookin' forward to it..." His voice trailed off, distracted by the strains of David Bowie singing *Life on Mars* coming from the jukebox.

I watched Terry stare across at his friend. You could tell he knew Frankie was madder than a rabid dog. I noticed the sharp intake of breath and the raised eyebrows as he pointed to me, listening in, and I met Terry's gaze with a hard stare. For some unknown reason he fortunately looked away. By studying them I could tell they were best friends, probably from school, and had served the same long prison sentences in the same prisons. I could also tell that Terry had no doubts whatsoever about Frankie and what he was capable of. Terry tugged Frankie's collar. "We've got enough to do tonight, so I don't want to be your babysitter, okay? If you want to give someone a kickin', do it in your own time. Tonight is strictly business, okay?" His voice was harsh as he fixed Frankie's mad gaze again.

Frankie half smiled, nodding. His eyes were fever bright and there was a steely glint in them. "You're the boss," he said with a dull hiss.

"Remember that," Terry hissed back.

As I continued to watch and listen I could tell that Frankie held Terry in great esteem, and could also tell that Terry had saved Frankie's bacon on more than one occasion – in and out of prison. Terry looked as hard as nails and was definitely the brains behind their daring-do. Brains were something Frankie obviously lacked.

Terry suddenly turned and stared doll-like at the barman. "I want another drink so, are you goin' to serve me or not?"

"Bar's closed!" said the other.

"Open it then!" snapped Terry, angrily rubbing out his cigarette on the bar top.

"Bar stays closed to you, mister," insisted the barman.

Terry snarled like an animal. "I want a drink! Don't make me ask again!"

I cringed for the barman's sake. My pinched face must have looked a picture.

"This is like listenin' to a fuckin' old radio show!" Frankie flared. He jumped up from his seat, pulling the Berretta from the black bag, pointing it at the barman's forehead. "Listen you thick bastard, you can't pick and choose who to serve or when to serve them. You're a fuckin' barman, not a politician or cultural attaché. So give my friend a drink," he insisted briskly.

"You're going to shoot me over a drink?" said the barman,

incredulously. His voice was deep and husky with a middle-class accent.

"I'm going to shoot you because I *can*," announced Frankie with a sneer.

"Relax," insisted Terry looking traumatised.

"Give my friend a fuckin' drink," said Frankie in an urgent whisper.

I saw the barman tremble, shaking his head with a terrified expression on his face.

"I'm gonna count to three," warned Frankie.

"Relax," Terry insisted again.

"One."

"Put the gun down for Christ's sake. You can't shoot him over a drink," said Terry.

"Two."

I watched the barman's face turn white as a sheet as Frankie cocked the gun.

"For Christ's sake, put the gun down!" Terry shouted.

"Three!" Frankie began to squeeze the trigger. "Be seein' yer," he said without any emotion.

I leapt out of my chair and made a grab for the gun. There was a deafening explosion as the weapon discharged a single 9mm round and the shell casing flew out of the chamber and hit Terry between the eyes. It bounced, rolling along the counter in what seemed to be slow-motion. The barman staggered backward, dropping to the floor like a slab of cold meat.

But there was no blood.

And he was still breathing.

Terry and his friend looked at each other and burst out laughing. "I think we'd better get out of here," whispered Frankie, "I've killed the fuckin' gumball machine!"

I stared at the smashed machine as they both ran from the

bar laughing. The barman staggered to his feet, looking bewildered. It was then that the old Times newspaper clipping of the event floated before my eyes. It had read: *The barman at Fat Jack's was brutally murdered today by a crazed gunman.* Yet he wasn't dead. So I had somehow changed the past again. My thoughts turned to Frankie. Was *he* my wife's killer? He was certainly capable of it and in the present day he was in jail – but denying all knowledge of any crime. However, I had seen him in action for myself. So, was he the one I was searching for?

Chapter 6
SOMEWHERE IN NORFOLK. ENGLAND. PRESENT DAY.

The guard moved his head closer to the small, smoked glass, bulletproof window, set in the heavy metal door. "What do you think it's made of?" he asked in a whisper.

"No one knows," said the other solemnly in a small voice. "They've tried to drill it with diamond tipped drills, cut it with lasers and blow torches, even used explosives charges like C4 – and nothing even dents or scratches it. It gives me the *creeps*. It just sits there staring straight ahead, but you know it's listening and waiting, probably for that single moment when it can reach out and grab you. It's begun to give me nightmares."

"Know what you mean, John," said the first guard. "I'd have sworn it blinked and moved yesterday. I'm just glad they've got it frozen and hope to Christ it never gets defrosted. Wish it was in a thick block of ice though. I'd feel much safer."

John recoiled from the wired window in horror. "Me too! Makes my flesh creep just looking at it! It has the same effect on everybody that comes to examine it. Scares 'em stiff, doesn't matter whether they're from the State Department in the U.S.A., or the British Air Force. They all come out of the padded cell with fear shining in their eyes. You couldn't get me to go in there, even if God walked in front of me!"

The other guard trembled, nodding. "Damn right, me neither. This whole thing reminds me of one of those old, black-and-white, scary *B movies* they used to show in the 1950's. But hard as it is to believe, it *is* really happening."

John moved his face back to the screen, pressing his nose right up to the cold glass. He seemed frozen. Hypnotized momentarily. *It is like a scary film,* he thought, *and hard to believe it's actually happening – but it is!* He tensed again as his eyes were drawn closer and closer to the thing's spectacularly grim metallic face, with those unblinking red laser eyes. Even though it seemed uncharged and weak, sitting there statue still, it seemed ominously menacing. *It's aware it's being watched and studied,* he thought. His heart began to race. However, he was completely compelled to keep watching, studying and doing what he didn't really want to do – take care of the thing.

Finally John moved away from the window, excusing himself. He walked down the long, dark hallway and crept into the loo, lowering the seat cover, sitting on it after pulling a magazine from his back pocket, strangely titled, *The Final Warning.*

Leaning back with his hands resting on his legs, clutching the magazine, he tried to concentrate on what he was reading but he couldn't sort out the confusion of thoughts swirling around in his head. He stared at the headlines: "Arson at college destroys whole campus: New board game could be perfect alternative to computer games: Car overturns trapping pregnant mother inside". Then he noticed the final headline: "Strange crater discovered on desolate marshy area in Southern Ireland". He looked at the date on the magazine. It was over a year old.

John was beginning to worry, sitting there in the quietness of the tiny room.

A loud rapping shook the door. "Are you going to be much longer, John?" asked the other guard.

John jumped as if slapped. "Sorry, I think I fell asleep," he said, deliberately taking his time to open the door as he flushed the loo.

Later that night, John pressed the button to draw the bullet-proof screens down over the windows outside the building and he glanced at his watch. It was one o'clock in the morning. A few moments later he was sitting in front of a CCTV screen with his cat purring contentedly on his lap, and as he stroked its soft fur with one hand he sipped a mug of strong coffee with the other. The second guard appeared from out of a door in the dark hallway and arranged the cushions in an armchair by John's side. He sat next to him and both stared at the TV images of the captured robot, and both felt a distinct coldness – a chill in the air.

"What do you think they'll do with it, Pete, when they've finished their tests?" asked John.

"Not sure," Pete shrugged, "but I've heard rumors that they're going to bury it in thousands of tons of concrete on a remote island somewhere in a specially built shaft, one thousand feet deep, just to be on the safe side. The government can't afford to have something like this running around loose if it ever comes to its senses."

The hairs on John's neck stood on end. "Do you think that will be an end to it?"

"There isn't anything that's capable of escaping from a concrete filled shaft, one thousand feet deep – I don't care what it is," said Pete rubbing his eyes. And as both men's tired eyes closed and they fell fast asleep – the robot's eyes opened.

***

IN LONDON I walked up and across an old stone bridge that spanned the gap over some disused railway lines, and although the mist had lifted slightly and the moon was shining, it was a black night, dark as pitch. After crossing the bridge, I trooped on down a grass verge by the side of the road, my boots and the bottoms of my jeans plastered in animal droppings and in a hell of a mess. But up the lane I trudged, past the occasional porch-light that had been left on burning brightly, casting eerie shadows to my rear.

At the end of the lane I turned to see if anyone was hiding in the shadows or following me, but the mist had closed behind me and I couldn't see any further than a few yards.

The rain had lessened now and moonlight was glinting off the water of the Thames River as I approached an old derelict building. *Jesus Christ, how much further,* I thought? *I'll be here when the devil comes to get me with his red eyes shining and his sunken cheeks smiling.* Actually, I don't believe in the devil and I'm not too sure about God either. I carried on walking through the light rain and at the end of another lane; I rounded a bend and came to a hotel. A flea-ridden looking place. I was standing at a wall next to a car park entrance, and there was a very old man dressed in yellow oilskins with a small yap of a terrier darting about in the weeds by the side of the road. The old guy was startled and looked up at me. "Dog needs a poo," he said, sounding embarrassed, smiling anxiously.

"I need a pee," I whispered, trying to make him feel at ease.

He quickly picked up the dog, placing it under his arm and disappeared back into the hotel from whence he came. I followed him into the hotel lobby. Inside it was dry, clean, warm and fresh, and somehow smelt of chlorine. I yawned and stared out of the window at the rain, then turned and caught my reflection in a nearby mirror. I looked like a rain lashed, windswept scarecrow.

I had followed Frankie and Terry from Fat Jack's bar, but lost the pair ten minutes later. *Now what,* I thought? And the only option seemed to be, to return to the present and start again if I had to, as the last few yards to make it to the hotel had been positively frightful. I was exhausted because I'd had great difficulty keeping up with Terry and Frankie – their feet were like quicksilver. *Did they know I was following,* I wondered? It worried me because they had at least one gun, and I only had the weapons that nature gave me – fists, feet and teeth. It wasn't exactly a fair fight if it came to it. I *was* afraid. Horribly frightened and don't mind admitting it. I trembled, the sudden realisation of my predicament hitting home.

Finally, I decided to take the safe option and go where I would be out of harm's way. I placed my hand into my coat pocket and took out the Time Machine, resetting it, pressing the button to take me back to the present day, and as usual, there was a breath of wind and the hotel lights glimmered and dimmed twice. Everything about me became indistinct. Ghostlike for a moment. And just before I vanished from the hotel lobby, the old man came back though the door without his dog, and he watched me disappear right before his disbelieving eyes, his face a picture never to be forgotten. He must have thought I was a *ghost*.

The noisy rushing feeling of time travel began and I blacked out for a moment after feeling ghastly and sick again as I returned to the cabin in Scotland and the present day. On arriving back I looked at the time. I had been gone mere seconds. Yet I had jumped back in time three years and spent a whole day there. I felt exhausted. Completely drained and worn out. So I put the machine away and went straight to bed, falling fast asleep the instant my head touched the pillow, and my dreams were the same as before – horrible nightmares, once again watching my wife die over and over again, while I was helpless to aid her.

***

THE NEXT MORNING, after getting up at 8:00am, I washed, shaved and dressed quickly, putting on casual clothes instead of my smart grey city suit. Blue jeans, a t-shirt and my old brown leather jacket were the order of the day; then I ate a breakfast of eggs and bacon with two slices of toast and a cup of tea. All very *English* you know, and the only thing I could think about was going back to Fat Jack's bar to start my quest for my wife's survival all over again. But then I thought, *why go back to the bar? Why not start my hunt for Terry and Frankie near the hotel where I lost them. That was a much better idea, because I wouldn't have to try and keep up with them and lose them again.*

Again I set the machine for July 25th 2008. But this time I set it for early evening and gave verbal commands that were very specific. I pressed the buttons and waited. In an instant, I had entered the Fourth Dimension and my mind went numb as the room spun wildly. Everything seemed to be a ghostly blur and I was sick to my stomach, feeling like a corpse awaiting life, but as I wandered further and further back in time I saw visions of cars, trains and airplanes, dishwashers, telephones and all the modern things that great minds had invented. Then I watched them smash into millions of pieces in one great collision and I passed out.

The next thing I knew, I had come to my senses and had both men in my sights, but then they disappeared again over a hill-crest into a thick wood that spread wide and black before me. Sadly, I'd lost them again and the twilight was deepening into night now. As darkness fell I looked back and found myself in front of the hotel wall, watching the old man in yellow oilskins with the small yap of a terrier darting about in the weeds. He looked startled again and stared up at me. "Dog needs a poo!" he said with a haunting familiarity, sounding embarrassed again.

"I need a pee," I said, eerily reliving the past. And just as before, the old man picked up the dog and scampered off into the hotel, disappearing upstairs. I followed him into the hotel lobby and slipped on the wet floor, falling to my knees, staring down at a freshly delivered newspaper. It was the late edition of the London Times. I gawped at the headline with disbelieving eyes. It read: "Barman senselessly shot dead in Fat Jack's bar by a crazed gunman".

But how could that be, I saved him yesterday, I thought? Then it hit me like a lightning strike. *No, I didn't. Today is yesterday! And I didn't visit the bar this time. I came straight here to the hotel, and I couldn't save him if I wasn't there!* With a sudden shiver my mind reeled in confusion. But now it seemed reasonable to assume that if indeed, I did change one moment in time, it would change everything else – a kind of knock-on, domino effect. And as the quiet of the evening crept over me, I went back outside, paused and put my hand into my pocket. Taking out the Time Machine, I stared at it in the dim light and its fluorescent dials glowed eerily in the dark like a ghostly face. I was missing something and I knew it, but I couldn't for the life of me figure out what it was.

I turned and stared at the tangled wood that Frankie and Terry had disappeared into and thought what it might hide. It seemed dark, spooky and very scary as the soft wind sung through the trees, because under that dense filigree of branches one might hide anything from the world – even from the sight of a million shining stars. And the leaves seemed to sigh and say, "Be careful where you go tonight!"

At this time my senses seemed supernaturally sharp, but unfortunately my feet seemed as if they were made of clay, for I wouldn't venture into that dark wood for all the tea in China or all the money in the world. Quite frankly, I was petrified and not just because Frankie and Terry had at least one gun that I knew about.

I hesitated, feeling tired, my feet in particular were very sore from the night before, and I was in doubt of what I should do next. Staring into that wood, my vivid imagination ran wild as to the lurking dangers: tree roots to stumble over;

tree boles to strike my head against and two crazed gunmen to stumble across, who would most certainly kill me without a second thought. And even though the woods seemed deserted except for the stirring of small living things and the night was very clear – no way was I prepared to venture further.

Pressing the required buttons on the machine I headed off in time, the noisy headlong rushing feeling beginning again, and I blacked out for a moment after feeling dreadful. When I opened my eyes I was materialising in front of the mirror, back in the cabin in Scotland, and watched my vaporous reflection reappear as if I were an apparition, flickering hazily into life like the night heat. I stared down at the old wooden clock on the mantelpiece. Once again very little time had elapsed, even though I had wandered back three years. Walking over to the bar, I poured myself a scotch and water and sat on the edge of the couch.

Did I know what I was doing? Did I really appreciate the magnitude of what I was getting into, I thought? My late wife's beautiful face drifted before my tired eyes. *Yes! Yes indeed! I knew exactly what I was doing and understood what I was getting into – or at least as far as I was able to, I did!* Fate had somehow intervened in my life by giving me something that, as far as I was aware, no one else had – a tiny machine with awesome power.

I was learning the art of time travel very slowly, one small step at a time, just like training for any given job, because unfortunately for me, there was no 'Fast-track' through this particular process. Then, I had a sudden thought regarding a wild possibility. *Had Einstein invented my Time Machine? Was that why the famous 'E=MC2' equation was on the third scrolling screen?* He was certainly fascinated by time travel, besides the motion of the universe, and had established certain theories and professed great knowledge on both subjects, saying that to travel through the Fourth Dimension was not only plausible, but actually possible. And when everyone else boohooed H.G. Wells' novel "The Time Machine" – written originally in the year 1895 – as utter shameless rubbish and pure fantasy, did Einstein not challenge them saying that they were *illiterate barbarians!*

Einstein certainly was one of the greatest minds of all time and proved it to the world on more than one occasion. For without him and his great genius there would have been no Atomic Age and fossil fuels will not last forever. Now I cannot but choose to wonder about the past, present and future, for the questions have been asked and discussed amongst us all, long before time as we know it began. Will we destroy ourselves? Will mankind cease to exist because of our vast ignorance? Or will we live on forever because of our strengths, convictions and pure faith in humankind. I could only hope.

I decided to test out the digital dials at the centre of the third scrolling screen, the ones with Einstein's equation underneath, because they were the only ones that I hadn't touched so far. How else could I find out what function they had? They were certainly there for a reason. I just didn't know what that reason was. However, it was late and I was tired, so I had another scotch and water and went to bed, where I had the weirdest dreams of what lay in wait behind those four tiny dials.

Chapter 7
SOMEWHERE IN NORFOLK. ENGLAND. PRESENT DAY.

Suddenly an alarm sounded. Heavy metal shutters came down over the grilled windows with a loud clank and the shrill noise of the intruder alert was deafening. Guards were running hither and thither, everywhere in panic. John stared with incredulity through the thick, bullet and bombproof smoked glass window. "The bloody things *gone*," he suddenly said, looking horrified. "It's bloody *vanished!*" The heavy, thirteen inches thick iron door was still tightly closed and locked and the glass intact. He stared through the small opening, visually scouring the chamber. Nothing had changed inside and there was no damage to the metal walls or ceiling, but the colossal robot had gone.

"It's impossible," John kept whispering to himself, mesmerized by the empty room. He blinked hard twice, hoping to see the thing back in its heavy metal chair. It wasn't. And the solid tungsten restraints were still unbroken. He shrugged. "How the bloody hell can I explain this to the higher authorities?"

Pete came running over to where John was standing. Being quite short, he strained and craned his neck to look through the smoked glass. 'Where's the bloody thing gone?' He looked dumbfounded and both men stared at each other without saying another word.

"One minute it was there and the next minute it wasn't," said a third guard from behind. "I was watchin' it, when it suddenly vanished right before my eyes!"

"But where's it gone?" said Pete. "Things don't just *disappear* into thin air!"

John looked bemused. "Don't know!"

Suddenly all the lights went out and the whole place

looked like a black hole. The three men took a deep breath and waited. Now the whole place was dark, spooky and very scary. A candle flickered into life and all three guards screamed at each other. A forth guard was standing in their midst, smiling. "I used to be a *Boy Scout*," he announced joyously, holding the candle in the air. "And I never go anywhere without a box of matches and one of these. Never know when you might need them." The three guards edged closer to their companion, feeling a little safer in the light.

"What the hell's happening tonight?" asked Pete. "First the alarm sounds, then we discover the robot's missing. Then the lights go out!" The guards edged even closer to the light. They were all quaking in their highly polished boots.

Suddenly there was a breath of wind and the candle flickered and went out. Immediately something grabbed at one of the men's clothes, scratching his bare skin. He reached out and touched something very hard and very cold, something metal. He screamed. They all screamed!

***

IN THE NOT SO DISTANT PAST, Terry looked up at the boiling mass of clouds sweeping across the sky. "Mother of God," he said. "Gonna piss it down!" The sky darkened, black clouds covering the sun; then it began to rain heavily in a drenching downpour. Terry and Frankie ran for cover under one of the great oaks surrounding them, desperately trying to shelter from the deluge. They had gone into the countryside for a relaxing day out, but at one point, Frankie had lost his temper – *BIG TIME* – in a village shop. He had been threatening and rude to the shopkeeper and customers, just because he had to wait in a queue to get served like everyone else. Terry had even stopped him from pulling out his gun.

Beneath the giant oak, both men glared at each other. "What the fuck is wrong with you Frankie? Can't you control yourself anymore? You've been running wild lately, like some fuckin' mindless aberration. You're out of control and I'm sick of bein' your fuckin' *babysitter*."

"I'm not out of control!" Frankie insisted.

"Yes, you fuckin' are! You were going to pull your gun and shoot the goddam shopkeeper, just because he wouldn't serve you first, for Christ's sake!"

"Well, he got me mad!" Frankie countered fiercely.

"For fuck's sake, if I went around shootin' everybody that made me mad, half the fuckin' City of London would be dead, includin' and especially you!"

Terry fell silent, unsure what to say next. He wasn't scared of Frankie but knew how explosive his temper could be. He'd seen it get the better of him on many occasions over the years, particularly in jail, and if anything it was getting worse instead of better. He sort of patted Frankie's shoulder gingerly. "Look, we've been friends for years, so take a little advice from me. Don't get so testy when you can't get your own way."

Frankie nodded, giving a crooked smile, the look of annoyance fading from his face. "I'll try. But I won't promise. Next you'll be telling me that patience is a virtue."

Finally the rain stopped and the sun came out, but as the day drew on, their interest in the countryside waned. So much so, that later that night after dark, they broke into the London Museum of Art and danced through gallery after gallery, impressed by the fact that they had broken in through sophisticated technology without effort, using nothing more than inferior burglary tools. They marched on through a long gallery filled with the finest paintings that Pablo Picasso, Renoir and Da Vinci had ever produced, sneering at them; saying that they were amateurish rubbish. They poked fun at the art and joked, drawing cartoon moustaches and beards on the great works while laughing madly, but what they didn't know was, that I was watching them in my spectre form, studying their every single move. Now I was finally one step ahead of them both. I watched them pass through another gallery with a vast array of idols – Grecian, Phoenician, Mexican and Polynesian, joking and poking fun at the tiny chiselled penises. Then they smashed the air-tight cases to pieces, ruining many of the priceless artefacts inside. Surprisingly, no alarm sounded. Had it not been set?

Much, much later that evening at about 2:00am in the morning, after they'd had their fill of fun – playing with wax dummies of cave men and causing small explosions with 9mm cartridges from their guns – they stole what little they could carry comfortably and left the museum by the same way they had entered, through a jimmied window. And in a "Eureka" moment, I followed them to their almost inaccessible hiding-place in that dark tangled wood, returning to the present greatly elated. Now I could hatch my plot against them.

Back in the present day, in Scotland, the Grandfather clock ticked away slowly, the noise of the swinging pendulum almost hypnotising me. I stood in front of the mirror above the hearth, staring down into the blazing fire and caught my own reflection out of the corner of my eye. I was smiling. But then, I was smiling on the inside too, and even though my mind was full of questions about time travel and what the possibilities were, I was now getting some positive results.

Not only had I altered time – as in my boxing career – but there had been no bad consequences so far. So could I fine tune things even more? I looked back at my life, at the long path I had taken and wondered if I might have visited myself in those times and changed anything, because time itself seemed to be such a paradox. I would only discover this with the passage of time.

I thought back to the night of my wife's murder. I had headed home from the office that night, tired and weary, having had a dreadful day in court like no other. Nothing had gone right and I'd had a bellyful of unjust law, because it was now a game of who could afford the most prestigious lawyer and nothing to do with guilt or innocence anymore.

I was unsettled that night, in a restless mood and went to bed early but couldn't sleep. I knew my wife was out with the girls in her office, but expected her home at a reasonable hour. I remember looking at my watch. It had been nearly four in the morning and she was still not home, so I laid thinking for ages, wondering where she was. However, I could never have imagined the awful truth.

She never came home, so I spent the whole of the next day ringing around friends and relatives trying to find her. Obviously I never did and no one knew where she was. She had disappeared on her way home, it was that simple. It was another full day before I found out the sickening truth. In the early hours of the next morning I had been rudely awoken, jumping to the sound of a pitiful, strangled cry – a woman's voice yelling out in terror.

Half asleep, I climbed from my bed, peering out of my window and could just make out a dark figure standing by the nearby fountain. Whoever it was, was small and thickset and moved about in a clumsy ungainly fashion. I remember looking around quickly, wondering what was happening, but by the time I looked again the person had disappeared into the misty night. Now I was curious. I had seen someone and heard a woman's cry.

I recall dressing quickly, making my way outside to the fountain via the front door, and there wasn't another soul to be seen. The street was now deserted. I stood for a few moments, transfixed, staring at some unknown object bobbing up and down in the water of the fountain, but it was dark and I couldn't tell what it was. It looked like a black football from where I was standing and I remember moving closer and closer, wondering if it was just a prank to wake me up and annoy me. But the closer I got to the fountain, the redder the water looked, even in the dark light.

I also remember glancing about sharply, stepping closer. The water *was* red. Then I noticed a woman's stockinged leg and a high heel shoe sticking out on the other side of the fountain bowl. Taking a deep breath, I leaned over and could make out the shape of a woman's black dress billowing about in the bright red water. I began to feel sick in the pit of my stomach, shrinking back for a moment. However, I pulled myself together. Taking another deep breath, I grabbed hold of the ankle and leg and heaved and the other leg appeared. Then the body. Seizing hold of the corpse, I hauled it out of the water, laying it on the ground. The woman's dress had ridden up over her head, hiding her face, but I had a feeling of dread because I recognised the clothes. "Oh, Jesus!" I cried out. "Oh, God, no!"

I was shivering now, but not from the cold. Pulling down the dress, I began to wretch, but was transfixed by what was a dual horror for me. The first was the gaping wound in the throat, which was from ear to ear and red against white skin. The second was her face. It *was* my wife Jane. And her body was still warm. I remember clenching my fists at the time and thinking, *who could do such a monstrous thing to a gentle woman – cut her throat and let her bleed and choke to death?* It wasn't until the autopsy a week later that I found out she had also been raped the night before, when she had gone missing.

My thoughts came back to the present and the soothing tick of the Grandfather clock. *No one should ever suffer such an appalling death,* I thought. Now I stood at the window in the shadowy early morning light and wondered what my next course of action should be. It was cold, grey and miserable outside, and that's exactly how *I* felt. The sky was masked in clouds and mist and the windows glistened from a steady downpour. However, at least there were no traffic jams and noisy neighbours here to distract me from my labours.

In a way, I felt like a detective in a murder mystery, but a detective with a difference. I was tracking down my wife's killer and was getting good at it, even though I was having to time travel to do it. *My story would make a good novel,* I thought. The journey was sometimes terrifying, but a marvelous experience in other ways, for I had chanced upon a secret key to the universe, which when I wanted it to, sent me on a roller-coaster ride through the vastness of time and space in a fast, racy, thrill-a-minute adventure. Or so it seemed!

The *Time Machine* seemed to be the world's most advanced computer – super-intelligent and super-sophisticated, besides being fantastic beyond belief in every manner possible. It opened up a whole new way of looking at the meaning of time and time travel. I used it constantly, over and over again, and found myself falling through the centuries like a smuggler searching for a treasure chest containing the secrets of the universe I also knew I was getting closer to the truth concerning Jane's murder.

The time-tunnel-vortex, or whatever it was the machine used to transfer matter across the ages, was so quick that I would black out briefly before entering a tunnel of bright light and emerge elsewhere, having the sensation of a great buzzing in my ears and a sharp pain in my head. It felt like being born – traumatic, yet amazing. And in some strange way, I *was* being reborn each time, because if you think about it, I belonged in another time era completely.

Suddenly, thunder rumbled overhead, startling me. I

looked out of the window at the black clouds rolling by and then something dropped through the front letterbox. I jumped again as I wandered down the dimly lit hallway and picked up the local newspaper delivered to my door. I stared down at the front page, scanning the columns of text with interest, but as always my mind was elsewhere.

I read the main headline about bombings in Afghanistan and wondered, *how people can continue to kill each other so casually and without a second thought.* And the one thing that struck me like being hit on the head with a brick and stood out in my mind, was the fact that bombs are very indiscriminate and impersonal killing machines. I could even imagine a bomber being able to detach their self from the act of killing, because he doesn't even have to be there. Whereas, the way my wife was murdered was up close and personal.

Chapter 8

What is time? Does it really exist? Have we a past, present and future? Or is time just a figment of our imagination? These are questions that I ask myself often and hypothesize the answers to. Here is another question I dwell upon. What if there were twins that grew to the age of twenty years old? And what if one of them left the earth in a spaceship at the speed of light, while the other remained on earth? In the succeeding years, which one would be the happier of the two? Well, I theorised the answer to this question with the aid of time, and therefore it must exist. The twin shooting off into space at the speed of light never seems to grow old – according to Albert Einstein's theories – and only has the experience of space travel. While the twin remaining on earth does age normally and have a full life with money, a wife, sex, children and a career to enhance his life. Therefore, I would imagine the latter to be the happier twin, all due to the passing of time.

Another interesting fact concerning time and indeed *space* is that most scientists are searching for intelligent life elsewhere in the universe, while *I*, without being sarcastic, am still searching for intelligent life on earth.

But once again, I digress from my story, so I'll cut my thoughts short. Dinner-time came and went and I decided on this dreary day, to write a very difficult letter to my children. I could feel myself frowning as I wrote it, and every now and then I stared up into space, trying to find the right words – helpful, not harmful ones. It was the most difficult letter I have ever written. How do you explain the unexplainable to your own kids? After reading my letter they will probably think me mad. Maybe I am mad – Mad as a Hatter!

I found myself writing, "*I love you both with all my heart, but there is something you need to know. It's unbelievable and is out-of-this-world, but true nonetheless. I have become a Time Traveller with a power beyond all reason, and I intend to use my Time Machine for the greater good. I'm not insane or trying to escape reality, however, I am facing up to it. I have written this letter just in case my plans fail and I am unable to make it back to the present day, and whatever happens, please don't think ill of me. Always keep in mind the good times we had together and remember me with fondness. I leave you my journal as some kind of proof that I'm not insane."*

Unfortunately, my letter babbled on, back and forth in what seemed to be a strange language even to me. I re-read it two or three times after writing it, and hoped they would understand the enormity of the words therein. Then, satisfied with my account of events leading up to the present day, I signed it, *'Your loving father'*. I sealed it in a manila envelope, placing it on the top of the drinks cabinet, ready for posting the next day. My kids were staying at my mother-in-law's in London while I was trying to sort my head out in Scotland.

With the letter written, I had places to go, things to do and people to see – but not in this century. Once again I was experimenting with time and time travel. You see, the Fourth Dimension intrigued me so much that I was actually willing to risk life and limb in the pursuit of truth and justice for my murdered wife Jane, who was beautiful, but vulnerable and helpless at the end of her life. There are some things that you just can't live without, and my wife is one of them. It's not money that makes the world go around, it's love, and Jane had more love than she knew what to do with.

And so, in the early twilight of evening, once again I said goodbye to the present day and slipped away from this century, through the dark starry night towards a distant century, on the road to the riches of knowledge with the aid of my Time Machine. I sighed as I travelled and must confess, I was on the verge of tears as old memories of my lost love flared in my skull, and visions of Jane floated before my eyes. Of course, I had to smile as fond memories unexpectedly entered my head too, with thoughts of us both living together to a ripe old age, while acquiring a sizeable fortune if given the time – but thirty-four years old is too young to die.

In my early experiments with the Time Machine, I thought *Time* was like a rainbow with the proverbial pot of gold at the end of it. However, I had to be careful on my travels through the Fourth Dimension, because it also seemed to be as faint and fragile as a butterfly's wings. If I accidentally caused the slightest ripple, I imagined that I could create a time paradox which might alter history in some catastrophic way. Whereas now, I know that time is quite *robust* and very hard to alter, even with the aid of my sophisticated shiny gadget.

So, I whisked off at the speed of thought to the far flung future, once again trying to find solace in the sunshine of our days, and as I roamed the centuries in seconds, I saw them as no more than a flicker – a glimmer, glimpsed in the blink of an eye like an amazing laser light show.

Stopping briefly every now and again to appraise the world around me, the changes time had caused never ceased to amaze me. There were mountains where once there had been valleys, blue waters instead of deserts, and some animals had only the vaguest resemblance to their long dead ancestors. Some creatures that had once lived above ground had become cave dwellers, while the cave dwellers had taken a liking to the sunshine and moved to the surface, and I couldn't help wondering how time managed it all as I only caught fleeting glimpses. I felt like an *immortal* that might one day choose death if I wanted to, but on my own terms, deciding the *when*, *where* and *how*, as I could take time literally and use it to my own advantage if I wanted to. And there seemed to be no greater power in the universe than mine, so I smile regularly now and congratulate myself because I'm unique!

***

NOT SO VERY FAR AWAY, in another time, Frankie and Terry were arguing like a couple of school kids.

"Why the fuck do you do that Frankie? You know it irritates me!" Terry barked.

"What?" sniffed the other.

"Pick your fuckin' nose and eat it! It's fuckin' disgustin' you twat!" spat Terry viciously.

"Don't know why I do it," Frankie mumbled faintly, wiping his nose on his sleeve. "But I always have!" A ripple of anger shot through him. He glared at Terry. "Anyway, it's my fuckin' nose and my fuckin' business, so I'll do what I want with it!"

"For fuck's sake, Frankie, it's bad enough pickin' your nose without fuckin' eatin' it!" Terry barked as they came upon a small cluster of well-to-do, fine looking homes nestled on a steep hillside. There was a small lake nearby with a boathouse perched on a wooden landing stage, and several rowing boats covered by a green tarpaulin bobbing up and down in the water. Suddenly, thunder rumbled and rain began to fall, spearing the lake as Frankie and Terry circled one enormous house stealthily on tiptoes, looking for shelter and some way to break in. Finally they came to a back door, and through a side window could see an old lady buttering bread on a kitchen table.

"She looks like my old granny," whispered Terry, smiling thoughtfully.

Frankie glanced at his watch, the dial glowing in the dark. It was almost midnight. "It's a funny time to be butterin' bread," he whispered back.

"She's probably doin' her old man's packin' up, ready for the mornin'," Terry guessed.

"They look filthy rich. Sinfully, filthy rich," Frankie snarled in a whisper.

"Don't look so heartbroken. You will be one day soon, if I have my way!" Terry announced, rubbing his hands together greedily, fluttering a smile as Frankie's eyes skipped away; searching for a weak spot in the downstairs windows.

That was their usual point of entry for smash and grab jobs, but these upper class residences would more than likely be alarmed, especially at night, so a more subtle approach was needed. The problem Terry faced was that Frankie hadn't got a subtle bone in his body. His way was like a bull in a china shop. If he saw it and wanted it, he would smash and grab it – and fuck the consequences!

"Come on, let's get on with it!" Frankie snapped impatiently.

Angrily, Terry's eyelids dropped and his face was pinched. "Keep your fuckin' voice down you moron or you'll wake the whole neighbourhood," he whispered. "We made plans and we're going to stick to 'em."

"For God's sake Terry, why can't we just break in now, do the old lady and get on with robbin' the place like we normally do?" Frankie's eyes shone fever bright.

"Because we'll end up nicked like we *normally* do, and I've done enough time for the both of us!" Terry countered as he spun on his heel and came nose to nose with his co-conspirator. "Now shut the fuck up and follow the plan!"

Frankie glared back at Terry, but didn't say another word. Suddenly, it began to pour with rain and both of them were drenched in seconds.

"Do you know something Frankie? Years ago I was a genius with a talent for making money and everything I touched turned to gold. But that was before I met *you!* Now everything I try to touch turns to *shit* before I can even get close!" Terry's eyes gleamed with anger and frustration as the cold rain ran down his face.

Suddenly, and without warning, Frankie knocked on the door. "This is the big bad wolf and his friend! Can we come in?" he shouted.

Terry was horrified. "What the fuck are you doin'?" he whispered. "Are you insane?"

The woman screamed and trembled. "Go away, whoever you are, I have a butcher's knife in my hand!" she shouted back.

Frankie laughed with genuine humour, tickled pink. "Eenie, meanie, miny, mo, will I stay or will I go!" he barked back, ignoring Terry and the woman. "Then let me in, for I'm a *butcher!*"

"I'll stab you in the heart if you come in!" screamed the woman, fear and fury bubbling inside of her. Then she heard Frankie laugh mirthlessly and froze.

"We just want to come in out of the storm!" Frankie teased, trying to frighten the woman a little more. "Open the door and let us in!"

"Go away or I'll call the police!"

"But you'll be dead by the time they arrive!" countered Frankie, laughing feverishly.

Inside the house the woman could see nothing beyond the glass of the window, but Frankie could see everything in the lamplight. He watched her move to the telephone, snatching it from its cradle.

"I wouldn't do that!" Frankie said.

"I am calling the police!" screamed the woman.

"But they won't get here. The roads are closed because of the storms, and we'll break down the door and kill you long before they arrive!" snapped Frankie.

Fear became terror and the woman froze again. She began

to sob pitifully and pray with tears streaming down her face. "What do you want?"

"Let us in and we'll look around, take what we want and leave. We won't harm you, I promise," Terry assured the woman in a calm voice.

"Open the fuckin' door or we will kill you stone dead anyway!" screamed Frankie.

The woman gripped the knife tightly with both hands. "No! Never!"

"What the fuck are you doing, Frankie," Terry snapped. "You're my curse and I've been lookin' after you most of my adult life. What the fuck has happened to you?"

Frankie laughed, smashing his fist through the window, showering the carpet in glass. The woman slumped back as Frankie climbed in, staring at her with mad, fever bright eyes. She bolted across the room to the door, fumbling at the lock. Frankie's hard hands grabbed her from behind and she screamed again as he lifted her from her feet. She lashed out but missed. Frankie released her, slamming her down into an armchair, looming over her. "Make this easy on yourself and let us take what we want." His mouth contorted into a sneer. "Then we'll..."

That was when the front door was kicked open, splintering the jamb. The woman winced and screamed. Terry was standing there with a 9mm Beretta in his hand, pointing it at Frankie. He cursed. "You're a dumb fuck! Now she's seen us both, so I've got to kill her, but I ought to kill you!" He cursed a little more, remembering his plan. A simple plan. *Wait until dark. Find the right house, a rich house. Break in at the dead of night, steal what we want and leave without violence. But Frankie complicates everything he gets involved in,* thought Terry.

He marched into the kitchen cursing and then launched forward, his fist colliding with Frankie's face, and the punch was so hard that the hysterical, sobbing woman thought his head might come off. He hit the stone floor like a sack of spuds. Out cold. The woman screamed as Terry loomed over her with impatient, but impartial eyes, pointing the Berretta at her head. "Drop the knife," he whispered.

The woman did as she was told, cowering beneath the barrel of the gun. "Please don't kill me. Please don't," she sobbed, pleading pitifully.

Outside, the sky was dark, grey and angry and the rain was lashing down. The kitchen door was blowing to and fro and then slammed shut in the high wind. "It's not a nice night to be out," said Terry calmly, his voice still a whisper. "But then, it's not a nice night to be in either, is it? You see, now I have a problem. *I* don't want to kill you, but *he* will when he comes to his senses. He doesn't have a conscience like me. He's madder than a rabid dog most of the time and very hard to control, so I can only do it if he believes that I'm worse than him. It's called mutual respect. I make the rules, he breaks the rules, but then he has to pay a price because I call the shots. And he's lying unconscious on the floor right now because he's just paid that price. He'll still break my rules in future, but at least he'll think twice first. So, what do I do with you?" he said awkwardly, glancing around the kitchen.

The house was big and quiet except for the steady tick of a Grandfather clock in a corner of the room and the woman's stifled sobs. Terry licked his lips and wiped them with the back of his hand. "You know, you do remind me of my old granny," he said finally, smiling uneasily. "And I'd not see any harm come to her." He helped the woman to her feet, said sorry for the broken window and door and the terrible fright, then he bid her goodnight. Hauling Frankie up over his shoulder he went out into the storm, leaving the old woman speechless – and lucky to be alive!

Chapter 9
SOMEWHERE IN THE FOURTH DIMENSION

Meanwhile, *I* was leaping from century to century, fine tuning my time-travelling skills, and I found that I could disappear from one time era and go anywhere in the blink of an eye. If *you* could do the same, where would you go and what would you do? Because with the Sat-Nav in my hands, I was armed with a power beyond all reason.

I decided to distract myself for a while and visit the 1930's – in particular, the gangster era of the Central United States. Being a lawyer, I had a passion to understand the lawless, and the lawlessness of the Great Depression interested me greatly. I tossed a coin. It was either go see Bonnie and Clyde or Lester Joseph Gillis, a.k.a., Baby Face Nelson. It was heads. Bonnie Elisabeth Parker and Clyde Champion Barrow won the toss.

I made the leap through the portals of time to *Rowena, Texas*. The date was October 1st 1910 and I watched Bonnie Parker being born, a traumatic violent birth to say the least. She was the second of three children, and her father – Charles Parker, a bricklayer of the time – was at the birth.

I made a second leap – to *Ellis County, Texas,* back to March 24th of 1909 – to watch her co-conspirator being born. It was an equally distressing birth. *Did this factor into their short violent lives,* I wondered.

With the aid of my Time Machine, I watched them grow up quickly, turning into well-known outlaws, robbers and criminals, who with their gang travelled and terrorised Central America between 1931 and 1934. Their exploits are well known and greatly documented, but I wanted to see for myself. I fast forwarded five major gun battles they'd had with the law, but never saw Bonnie pull or fire a gun. That was one myth exploded there and then.

Clyde, however, relished the thought of pulling and firing a gun, and I saw the insane glare in his eyes when he did. He also cracked safes, robbed stores and stole cars with the same relish, but was primarily known for robbing banks. I watched him do all of the above and he loved every minute of it, telling the newspapers he was seeking revenge against Texas for his abuse in their prison system while serving time. His favoured weapon was the M1918 Browning Automatic Rifle.

I watched things get even uglier when Buck Barrow joined the gang in 1932. The whole gang was on the run together in August, while Bonnie was visiting her mother. Clyde, Buck and an associate were drunk at a dance in Stringtown, Oklahoma when they were rounded upon by a sheriff and his deputy. All three opened fire, killing the deputy, Eugene C Moore, and it was the first killing of nine law men by the Barrow Gang.

Being a pacifist myself, I needed to understand the thought processes of a killer if I was to save my wife's life.

The Barrow Gang now consisted of Bonnie and Clyde, Buck and his wife, W D Jones, Raymond Hamilton and Henry Methvin, and stories of their encounters with the law became almost mythical. Yet it's true that they were both *reviled* and *adored* by the public, because notoriously they would shoot anyone who got in the way of their escape – whether civilian or lawman. However, despite their glamorous image, they were all desperate and discontented criminals just like Terry and Frankie in their time era.

As my spectral self, I watched another shoot-out. Buck Barrow got shot in the side of his head and died of his wounds in Platte City in July of 1933, and I watched Blanche Barrow getting jailed in Missouri following his violent death. Then I saw the law finally close in on the Barrow Gang in May of

1934 on a desolate road near Bienville Parish, Louisiana.

At exactly 9:00am that morning as Bonnie and Clyde's stolen Ford V8 approached me, a posse concealed in the bushes opened fire with Browning Automatic Rifles, shotguns and pistols, emptying everything they had into the car. I never heard the posse call out a warning or an order to surrender. Instead they pumped one hundred and thirty rounds into the car in a frenzied attack. I saw Clyde killed instantly from a head shot, but Bonnie wasn't so fortunate. I heard her long horrific screams as the bullets tore her apart, the officer's emptying everything they had into her and the car. I was violently sick and leapt back to the present, not understanding what I'd just seen. Had I witnessed *justice* or a *murder?*

My wife's horrific murder came back to haunt me in my head. I've been a lawyer for twenty-five years and there is nothing wrong with justice, so long as the right people get put away or executed. But most killers' gets their sentences squashed down from murder to second degree manslaughter, and there is something definitely wrong with that, because sometimes vengeance *is* justice and that *is* an unalterable fact!

I was hooked and needed to see and know more, as distressing as it was, so I leapt back to December 6th 1908 to watch "Baby Face Nelson" being born. It was another traumatic, violent birth. He was born in Chicago's Near West Side, to a middle-class family of Belgian immigrants. I fast forwarded to Christmas Eve of 1924 and watched his father Joseph commit suicide. Baby Face was just sixteen years old then, but already in reform school, arrested for theft and joyriding. He was a petty thief into his late teens and had rumoured connections to the notorious gang leader Al Capone, but I saw no evidence of this as I shadowed him in my ghostly form. He did, however, finally partner up with Public Enemy Number One – John Dillinger.

In contrast to Dillinger, *Baby Face* was the antithesis of his Robin Hood-like partner, gangster, having a tendency to let his wild temper overcome him, and Nelson didn't hesitate to kill innocent bystanders or law-men. Yet strangely, he was a devoted husband and father who usually had his family with him while running from the law.

As you might imagine, after Dillinger was shot dead outside the Biograph Theatre in Lincoln Park, Chicago in July of 1934, Nelson became Public Enemy Number One and boasted to the news media about robbing a bank a day for a month, outdoing Dillinger. This was more than enough to get him noticed by the head of the FBI – J Edgar Hoover.

Following a shoot-out at the secluded Little Bohemia Lodge near Rhinelander, Wisconsin, Nelson was identified as a member of the Dillinger gang after killing federal agents W. Carter Baum and J. C. Newman. That's when he became nationally notorious and a high priority target for the FBI.

I shadowed his trail and watched him procure a bullet-proof vest as the odds began stacking up against him, and saw it save his life more than once. Outside one bank he exchanged fire with a local jeweller, who shot him in the chest ineffectively because of the vest. The merchant was lucky that day. He retreated into his store under a hail of bullets from Nelson; however, time was now running out for the gangster.

It finally did at the so-called *Battle of Barrington* incident – a running gun battle between FBI agents and Nelson on November 27th of 1934. I watched the incident begin when Nelson, his wife and an associate were driving down a long lonely country road and they spotted a car with two known FBI agents going in the opposite direction. Nelson hated the law, any law, and recognising them, swung his car around and gave chase. In close pursuit he opened fire on the agents, shattering both wind-shields and the driver fought for control of the car and swerved, avoiding an oncoming milk truck, but wound up in a field. Nelson swerved his car into the entrance of Barrington's North Side Park, slamming on the brakes.

I watched incredulously from my ethereal vantage point as Nelson exited his car and began walking towards the agents' car shouting, 'I'm gonna kill you sons of bitches!' And he opened fire so rapidly with a .351 rifle that I mistook it for a machine gun.

One of the agents exited their car and dived into a ditch across the road. Turning to aim his machine gun at the gangster, he fired two or three bursts, but then his weapon jammed and failed and he fell in a hail of bullets from Nelson. Immediately, the other agent exited their car, firing a shot gun blast that struck Nelson in the legs, knocking him over, but amazingly he climbed back to his feet and kept coming at the agent, who fled across the road. Then the agent turned and tried to discharge his weapon unsuccessfully as it was empty. He too fell under fire from Nelson.

I watched Nelson calmly, even casually, stride over to the agent and blow his brains out. Once again I was violently sick. Striding over to the other downed agent, he riddled his body with bullets just to make sure *he* was dead and laughed like a mad-man. But then, he was a mad-man, and a dying man, because for once he wasn't wearing his coveted bullet-proof vest and had been hit nine times in the arm, legs, chest and stomach. However, he still managed to flee the scene with his wife and associate and drove to a safe house where he died in bed several hours later. I watched all of this happen and then wandered back to the present day and the cabin in Scotland.

Finally, I understood the mind of a murderer. Nelson, like Bonnie and Clyde were psychopathic killers with no conscience, no morals, no sense of good or bad, right or wrong. I saw the same traits in Frankie – but not in Terry.

I had been at the cabin in Scotland for just under a week when I decided to propel myself back three years again; to the awful night of my wife's abduction and murder. I now knew and understood a lot more about the Time Machine and its complex working. *But did I know enough?*

I leapt back to Fat Jack's bar on the night my wife went missing, and this time I was in a solid form. Walking around the red brick exterior I leaned against it, the brick rough and cold against my face. The wind was icy, the sky clear and stars were sparkling brightly like tiny diamonds overhead. Suddenly, there were footsteps on the walkway behind me, and I turned, hunched, glancing back, watching Terry and Frankie approaching. My blood chilled because Frankie was laughing, but both passed by without noticing me in the shadows. Frankie's face, however, shone in the direct glare of the red neon lights of the bar window and he looked crazier than ever, the red hue making him look like the *devil*.

I had done my research and found out from police reports that this was the last bar my wife was seen in alive, and Frankie and Terry were the last customers to leave the bar, seconds after my wife and her best friend Vicky left. That spoke volumes to me, having seen what the pair were capable of doing. Now, images and sounds exploded before my eyes and in my mind – the shooting of the barman in Fat Jack's, which I had subsequently changed with the help of my Time Machine. The terrified face of the woman they were going to rob and kill in the farmhouse. The maniacal laughter echoing throughout the museum they had broken into. And all of it seemed so unreal, like a ghastly nightmare.

Nevertheless, it *was* a stark reality! I came back to myself, still leaning on the wall. Then the *EXIT* door to the bar slammed open, hitting me like a jack-hammer in the back and I slid down the wall, ending up sprawled on the concrete as a huge coloured guy brought out the trash and dumped it in the alleyway right in front of me. "You okay?" he asked, looking down at me, slightly perturbed.

"No... I'm bloody well not, you clumsy oaf!" I said, staggering back to my feet, brushing myself down.

He glared at me and snarled, "Shouldn't be standin' there in the first place... idiot!" He went back inside, slamming the heavy metal door shut behind him.

I walked back around the corner, staring at the fluorescent dial on my watch, shining in the dark. It was now midnight. Suddenly, a black cab pulled over to the curb and screeched to a halt. The door flung open immediately and my wife and Vicky jumped out. I ducked back into the shadows of the alleyway before they could see me, but it was so strange seeing her standing there *alive,* paying the cab fares, when three years hence in my present – she was dead. My eyes misted, tears rolled down my cheeks and the lump in my throat made it hard to swallow as old memories of the great times we'd shared flared in my mind. I had to push them consciously to one side.

My feelings were still raw and hurt like hell, but there she was large as life and even more beautiful than I remembered. That's the trouble with the passing of time; beautiful memories fade and cease to exist like grains of sand slipping through your fingers. I couldn't stand it. I went back to the present day; however, just before I made the leap, I would have sworn I saw something huge, made of metal glinting in the shadows of the alley behind me, with two glaring red eyes staring my way.

Chapter 10
STIRLING. SCOTLAND. PRESENT DAY.

Back in Scotland, one day later, I set out with fresh purpose, my confidence growing. I knew I could visit the past, present or future in my solid or spectral form, and also knew I could influence any one of them at any time. However, I needed to be able to tweak them a little, like fine tuning a favourite TV show – get rid of the static blurring my vision, so to speak.

I thought back to my wife's funeral. It had been the saddest day of my life, and my children's. The Cross Lane funeral parlour was packed to the rafters with grave-faced people who glided past me quietly in dark clothing, nodding reverently, knowing that I was the husband of the deceased. Then family and close friends viewed the open casket. I did too. God, she looked so beautiful. It was just as if she were sleeping. The funeral parlour make-up artist had done us proud. She looked like Snow White and somehow, even in death she was a million times more beautiful than I had ever seen her in life. So peaceful! *Goddamnit all to hell! I wanted to run away and hide for the rest of my life.* I cried like a baby. Great racking sobs that I couldn't stop.

I came back to myself, but have you ever tried to swallow a big, dry pill? That's just how my throat felt by thinking about my wife. It was like a big piece of bone lodged in my throat and I couldn't get rid of it. I took a deep breath, then another and swallowed hard. I was sick to my stomach and my heart was racing with rage for the one who had murdered the gentlest, most selfless woman I ever knew.

My wife was cremated that day and the urn engraved with a short poem she had written for me, some days before she was taken from me.

It read:
> *Regrets I have*
> *But very few,*
> *For within is locked*
> *My love for you,*
> *Silent,*
> *Ever faithful,*
> *Forever true to thee,*
> *I cannot live*
> *Without your love,*
> *For your love is*
> *Life to me...*

I read it again and again and cried for hours. I was scared that day, of a life that lay ahead of me without her, and I'm still scared now. Angry too. And every day that passes since her death I get angrier, even when I sob quietly in bed at night so as not to wake the kids.

My mind snapped back again. I glided over to the drinks cabinet and poured myself a scotch with a splash of soda water. Sitting down on the couch, I stared at the Time Machine. Other than meeting my wife and having kids, it's the best thing that's ever happened to me in my entire life. I stared at the machine intently, scrolling and studying its many screens, but my wife's face kept drifting into my mind like a ghostly face – focusing clearly and then floating away. I even seemed to hear her voice saying: *You have the machine now, you can save me! You can!*

I answered: *Sweetheart, wherever you are, I AM trying to save you! I am! I promise... and if it's at all possible with this machine... I'll succeed!* Then the tears came again and great racking, irrepressible sobs tore from my throat. I stood up and went to the drinks cabinet, pouring myself another scotch and water, wiping my runny nose with the back of my hand. I hadn't cried like this for three years. *God damn it all to hell!*

I'd had the world at my feet three years ago as a successful lawyer, running my own practice with a great life and a beautiful wife and kids, but I can barely remember those days now. *Christ, how I miss you Jane.* The tears came again. Then for a single moment I could smell her heady rosewater perfume, and it was as if she had joined me from somewhere beyond the grave. It was disconcerting to say the least, but quite comforting in a way. Then a small voice in my mind said, *See you soon darling.* It faded into silence.

Love hurts. I sipped my scotch, staring through the golden liquid, drumming my fingers on the crystal glass. I was angry still and decided to pass the evening reading to calm myself down. I picked up an old journal lying in the paper rack. It was a *London Times* supplement and the glossy front cover announced: THE LAST MOMENTS OF A GOLIATH. It was a journal about the sinking of the R.M.S Titanic, which was probably the worst sea disaster with the greatest loss of life to date. I began to read with interest, even though I knew most of the facts surrounding the ship's sinking, and though my eyes were heavy like lead. I glanced at my wristwatch and it was almost midnight.

The main headline of the journal read: "TITANIC SINKS FOUR HOURS AFTER HITTING ICEBERG..." and the text reported: "866 rescued by Carpathia, probably 1250 perish. Ismay safe, Mrs. Astor maybe, noted names missing." It went on to admit that the Titanic, the biggest steamship in the world, had been sunk by an iceberg and gone to the bottom of the Atlantic Ocean in less than two hours, probably taking more than 1400 passengers and crew with it – a disaster of huge proportions!

I was getting more tired by the minute and beginning to fall asleep, however, I read on for quite some time, even though I was drowsy and my head beginning to swim.

Then I had an idea. Why not leap back in time and see if I can stop the disaster from happening? I'd changed my boxing career, and I now knew more about the Time Machine's working, so it might be possible. It was worth a try at least. If I leapt back in a solid form I could warn the captain of their impending doom. Whether he would believe me is another matter entirely!

I went and washed my face in cold water, then to my wardrobe and dressed quickly, slipping on a dark grey suit, black shoes, a heavy fur lined coat with a woolen scarf about my neck. I was *good to go* in moments, Time machine at the ready. Turning it on, the familiar static buzzing hissed in my ears and vibrated my hands. I set the dials in sequence to late afternoon of April 15 in 1912 and punched in the coordinates given by the journal of the Titanic's last known position in the Atlantic. If they were wrong, I would probably leap back in time and fall into the freezing sea and die without a trace. So I decided to err on the side of caution and travel back as my spectral-self first, to make sure the great liner was there. I clicked onto SPECTRAL and pressed the GO button hesitantly. The buzzing from the machine grew louder and louder, the vibrating stopped and then I was off at the speed of thought, travelling through the wormholes of time – if indeed that's what was making my journey possible.

Instantly, my mind reeled in a kind of fog and once again I felt the strangest sensation, one of flying, but looking about me it seemed like nothing was happening. Then I noticed my reflection disappearing from the mirror above the fire like an elusive ghost, drifting off.

After a short period of feeling nauseous and ghastly, everything went black and the awful sickly feeling was replaced by a falling sensation. Suddenly, there was a flash of blinding light and a great confusion of noise around me as I opened my eyes. I had done it. I was there, back in time, standing on the promenade deck of the Titanic as my spectral self with passengers all about me. I glided to a hidden place behind one of the life boat davits and pressed the *SOLID FORM* button on the machine.

Instantly, I felt the sensation of my body weight return, a rush of blood to my head and there was wind whispering in my ears. The air was freezing and tiny flakes of snow were drifting down from the heavens as I watched the breath of passengers wafting up into the air. It was definitely late afternoon in early April and the sun was just setting, leaving a glorious orangey hue across the horizon.

I turned to look out to sea and it wasn't blue. It was almost black; the temperature well below freezing and it glistened. Ominously it was dotted with icebergs, even though only small ones the size of houses and some sporadic pack ice. Turning again my attention wandered, and I cast my eyes over the shadowed faces of the passengers, well-heeled people dressed in expensive clothes and swathed in jewellery.

Suddenly, chunks of ice slammed against the ship, shaking her. I shivered from the cold, despite my heavy fur-lined coat and scarf, watching a nearby iceberg shedding huge chunks of ice which tumbled against each other, falling with a great creak and crash amid roiling black waters. More chunks of ice slammed into the ship, shaking her and I jumped as if slapped; turning my head and a beautiful woman caught my gaze. It was Mary Astor. I recognised her from the journal, her plump cheeks were red with cold but she smiled at me kindly. "Don't worry too much about the ice hitting us, this ship is the unsinkable Titanic," she whispered softly with an air of confidence, her hair gathered together beneath a hood set with pearls. *How wrong she is,* I thought. She smiled again and slid away.

Now my attention was drawn to the sound of Jazz music coming from somewhere inside the ship's great hulking carcass. I noticed it as soon as it started because I hate Jazz. Pacing the length of the promenade deck, I followed the sounds until I came to a door with a sign which read: *THE COOLING ROOM AND TURKISH BATH*. Directly across from the sign was the ballroom with its ornate golden doors open, and I could hear and see the band playing and people dancing. I looked up at a sign above my head. A green arrow pointed and announced: *GRAND STAIRCASE LEADING TO FIRST CLASS DINING SALOON*. It pointed to a staircase leading two floors below deck, so I descended rapidly.

Reaching the bottom, another green arrow pointed the way to the dining saloon, so I headed in the direction indicated, passing a barber's shop, a photographer's darkroom, a clothes pressing room, a lending library and the wireless operator's room, until I reached two ornate silver doors. Placing my hands on the handles I levered both of them open. Standing for a single moment, I listened to the buzzing conversation and stared in awe at a vast room that carried on into an upper level, ending in a domed skylight. Glancing around the room I tried to locate the officers table and spotted it almost immediately. Captain E J Smith was at the head of the table with officer Lightoller to his left.

Suddenly, I began to feel light-headed and strange – nauseous even. Then a great weariness overcame me and I couldn't understand what was happening, until the Time Machine in my coat pocket began to vibrate and buzz. Placing my hand into my pocket I took it out, staring at it. To my dismay, the machine was indicating a low battery warning and announced that I only had ten minutes left before the battery would fail. In my damned hurry, I had forgotten to recharge it.

The horror of this revelation hit me like a hammer. I was now on the Titanic and it was going to sink in a few hours. Without the Time Machine I would be stranded here and probably go down with the ship, and I hadn't brought the charger with me.

I took two or three deep breaths; shook my head and began pushing and prodding my way forward through the milling passengers towards the captain's table, while he and his officers were all sitting with their backs to the wall, each one eating a beef dinner of generous proportions. The Yorkshire puddings, mixed vegetable and thick gravy looked amazingly appetising and smelt delicious wafting gently my way.

As I walked I slipped my hand inside the pocket of my overcoat and pulled out the journal, holding it firmly, looking at its smooth front cover with the undeniable facts emblazoned there. *But even with this as proof of the ship's dire fate and what is to be, no one will believe me... that much you can bet on,* I thought.

I walked on with purpose, picturing the horrific scene of the ship settling beneath the waves like a giant leviathan dying. To this day I don't believe my imagination could do justice to such a scene, even though I could hear the awful screams in my mind. I headed straight for the captain, staring into his dark eyes as he looked up from his meal and caught my gaze. Then I stared down at my watch. I had less than eight minutes to go before the Time Machine would fail. My experiment was going terribly wrong and I wasn't learning from the experience. Every attempt to change the past had failed except for two – my boxing career and the shooting at Fat Jack's bar – and I couldn't figure out why.

The headline on the journal about the Titanic sinking was compelling evidence, yet I knew no one would believe it, or me, even with my most desperate efforts to convince them. Obviously in the present day it was an up-to-date fact that most people knew about, however, would *you* believe a stranger who walked up to you and said he was a Time Traveller from the future? I think not! I know I wouldn't!

The captain stared, looking me up and down, waiting for me to reach his table and speak, obviously thinking that I was just another passenger who was going to congratulate him on his promotion to captain of the greatest liner ever built, and the running of a tight ship. But for me, there was a kind of breathtaking suspense, because I had no idea what I was going to say to him. Yes, I had proof – the journal – but from the future?! Come on, be realistic! "It's a fake and you are a charlatan and crazy if you think I will fall for such an outlandish confidence trick. What do you really want? Why are you here?" he will say.

Well, things never turn out the way you expect them to and I never expected to be here on the Titanic, not in a million years. However I am, and for the best reason in the world – to try and save hundreds of lives. So, I took two or three deep breaths and carried on walking towards the dining table and the captain, trying to fix keywords for my argument into my head. Then, one word jumped into my mind unexpectedly – psychic. *Maybe the captain would believe I'm a psychic. It's a freaky idea, but maybe, just maybe he might, whereas there's no way on God's green earth he'd believe I'm a Time Traveller!* I looked at my watch again. I had less than five minutes before the Time Machine would fail, leaving me trapped in the past on a ship that was doomed and soon to sink.

The captain broke away from my gaze and carried on eating. It was hard to believe that fifteen minutes or so ago, I was in the cabin in Scotland, and the biggest problem I had was that I'd forgotten the can-opener for the tins of beans I'd bought. How strange is that?

I was just about to speak, when I glanced up to see my own reflection in a mirror on the wall behind Captain Smith. Somehow I looked like a rabbit caught in the glare of car headlights and I stared at my face, realising I'd forgotten to shave because I'd been in too much of a hurry to get on with the experiment at hand. My gaze wandered back to the captain's face as I rapped my knuckles gently on his dining table, coughing loudly to get his attention. "Good evening!" I greeted in a sort of thoughtful way. "Would it be possible to have a polite word with you gentlemen, for I have something rather disturbing to put to you?"

The captain looked up from his meal again and nodded. He pointed to a chair, bidding me to sit. My whole body stiffened. I felt like throwing up. Like running away. I moved to the chair uneasily, feeling a presence behind me as I sat down. It was one of the stewards. "Would you like a glass of wine?" he asked in his stiff upper-lip English accent. I shook my head and he carried on filling the officers' glasses and then left the table. I closed my eyes for a moment, thinking that my time was running out. Soon the battery in my Time Machine would be exhausted. I opened my eyes. Every one of the officers awaited my words. *Where the hell do I start?* Turning to face the captain I took a deep breath and stared into his eyes as his brows lifted expectantly. "Well?" he asked; his tone deep and resonant.

"I've no idea how to approach the subject on which I'm about to speak, other than to say it plainly, so I'm here to tell you that this great liner of yours is going to collide with a colossal iceberg tonight, and sink in less than two hours to the bottom of the Atlantic, taking almost fifteen hundred souls with it!" I said it like a man with verbal dysfunction and must have looked embarrassed saying it, even though it was true. I felt my face flush and colour up, even though it was cool in the dining room, but I was hot under the collar and sweat ran between my shoulder blades.

The captain looked like he'd been slapped in the face at first, but then he began to laugh with great gusto. The other officers began to laugh too. Funnily enough, I figured that's exactly what they would do, however they would have laughed harder and longer if I had told them I was a *Time Traveller*, even though that was true too! Sitting there with a straight serious face, I waited until the cheerfulness faded.

"It's not April 1st again, is it, because..." the captain inquired flippantly with a wry smile.

"No, sir, it isn't!" I interrupted curtly. "It's April 15th of 1912 and this ship *will* strike an iceberg and sink as surly as the sun will rise again tomorrow morning!"

The captain's bushy, bearded face suddenly became serious. "How could anyone possibly know such a fact, even if it were true? You're talking about a future event. Are you a *Time Traveller*, sir, with actual, factual proof? Are you going to produce a future newspaper from your pocket with a report of the disaster and great loss of life?"

I laughed inwardly. *I could do just that! But you wouldn't believe that either,* I thought. "No, sir, I'm a psychic, a clairvoyant with a proven track record. However, I have no concrete evidence of what is about to befall this ship," I enlightened in my most serious tone.

Every one of the officers looked around the table at each other and then settled on the captain, awaiting his wise words and his reaction to my statement. "A psychic, eh? Well, it's more credible than a *Time Traveller*," he said finally.

I couldn't believe my ears. Was he actually open-minded enough to believe that such people exist? He smiled a little smile. Then he shook his head, raising his bushy eyebrows.

"I'm a rational man who believes that anything is possible..."

I breathed a sigh of relief.

"... Anything except time travel and being able to see into the future, because for me to believe those concepts I would certainly need irrefutable evidence as proof! Both are preposterous ideas, born in the mind of a science fiction writer, surly to God!" His tone was sarcastic.

My heart sank as I glanced nervously at my watch. *Only one minute before the time machine fails, stranding me on a death ship.* It was time for desperate measures. If I was to change captain Smith doubts, I had to give him his irrefutable proof. And what better way to do it than to disappear right before his disbelieving eyes, and the eyes of his officers. *Well seeing's believing, isn't it?*

"So, you want undeniable proof before you believe in something?" I said, pulling the Time Machine from my inside pocket.

FORTY SECONDS BEFORE THE BATTERY DIES...

I set the dials for present day Scotland with the appropriate coordinates.

THIRTY SECONDS...

The machine began to buzz and vibrate, warning me that my time was almost up.

"Captain Smith, this ship *will* sink tonight!" I barked, commanding everyone's attention. "However, you can stop it from happening by slowing the ship down and striking the iceberg head on!"

TWENTY...

My mouth was bone dry suddenly. I was cutting this fine. But it meant saving the lives of hundreds, balanced against my own fragile existence. I had to risk it!

TEN...

"Look at me captain. I'm not a figment of your imagination, am I?" I rapped my knuckles hard on the table. Hard enough to tear my skin and draw blood. I placed the same hand palm down, leaving a bloody print on the table cloth when I lifted it again.

FIVE...

The time machine was now buzzing loudly and vibrating so much that it was shaking my hand.

"Captain... you *are* going to die tonight unless you heed my warning!" I announced stiffly, pushing the journal into his hands.

ONE SECOND...

The screen on the machine began to fade. I pressed the red button to go back to the present day and safety. Nothing happened. I didn't leap. *Shit!* I pressed it again. Nothing happened. *Shit!* I pressed it a third time, really fast and really hard, waiting for what seemed like a lifetime. The captain stared at me, wondering what I was doing. What was I doing? Nothing was happening. The battery in the machine had failed and *I* was still on the Titanic.

Panic flooded through me. I had no idea what to do. *I'm going to die tonight,* I suddenly thought. I stood up straight, speechless. Then, I noticed my reflection disappearing from the mirror above Captain Smith's head, drifting off like a ghost. I glanced at the Time Machine's face. It lit up fleetingly and faded again with the last dying spark from the battery. My heart was beating fast and it seemed hard to catch my breath, being nervous and afraid, and the last thing I saw before everything went black and I passed out, was captain Smith's disbelieving gaze staring at me as I vanished right before his eyes.

Chapter 11
STIRLING. SCOTLAND. PRESENT DAY.

I woke up in the cabin in Scotland, lying on the lounge carpet, listening to the steady tick of the Grandfather clock, my mind dizzy. I puzzled matters through when my mind was right. Had I really used the Time Machine, wandered back to April 15th of 1912 and actually walked the decks of the greatest steamship of our age? The very thought was incomprehensible, surreal, and I didn't know for sure. To be honest, I wasn't sure about anything anymore, because the last couple of weeks had become a blur, a kaleidoscope of activity as I wandered through time into the unknown and returned unharmed. I shuddered at the thought because I could have been killed more than once.

Rolling to my knees I climbed to my feet, shaking my head as I walked unsteadily over to the wall bar. I made myself a drink, my usual scotch on the rocks with a splash of water. Measuring it out, I sipped at it and it was good, just what I needed. Sitting down on the couch I lifted my legs up, trying to relax, but all I could think about was whether Captain Smith had heeded my warning. I chewed gingerly on the inside of my lip, needing to know if I had made a difference.

I glanced at my wristwatch. It was a couple of minutes past midnight and I'd been gone a considerable length of time, yet hardly any time had elapsed at all in the present day. *Why didn't this damn thing come with an instruction manual,* I thought? *What exactly happens when I leap through time? And why do I never materialise inside solid objects or smash into things?* I wanted to know. No, I needed to know! Because every time I made a leap, it went against all of my natural instincts. I remembered reading about Albert Einstein and his theories and understood most of them, but they didn't seem to apply to *Time Travel*. I paced around the room trying to remember things, such as my first leap through time; however it was all a blur now.

It was really late, but I decided to ring my mother. *No, relax, it's too late, tomorrow will be soon enough. I've been treading a tightrope for quite a while now, so a few more hours won't matter or make that much difference.* I was tired and my mind was shutting down, so I decided to head off to bed.

***

AFTER SLEEPING HEAVILY it was lunchtime of the next day before I woke up and called mom. "Hello sweet, how are you today?" I inquired, her image flashing in front of my eyes, smiling.

"I'm fine Ben. How are you these days?" she said almost reluctantly.

My heart sank. "You don't sound happy to hear from me mom," said I swallowing hard.

"Have you been to see Dr. Aldrich recently?" she asked hesitantly.

I blinked and flinched. "No, I'm beginning to control my emotions without him!" I countered defensively. "I'm still full of hate and anger, but learning to control it." The image of Jane's broken-doll body in the fountain with her throat cut from ear to ear and blood everywhere flashed through my mind. I blinked back the tears and swallowed the lump in my throat, which was suddenly bone dry. The pain surfaced sharp and ragged as I saw Frankie and Terry's faces laughing madly, looped endlessly over and over and over in my mind. I shook the vision from my inner eye. *Shit! I thought I'd worked my way through this.* I held my breath, my mind numbed and dizzy.

"Mom, I need to ask you something that might sound strange," I suddenly blurted, shifting uncomfortably from one foot to the other.

There was a fleeting silence at the other end of the line. "Okay, fire away!" she said.

"What year did the Titanic sink, can you remember?" I asked, hoping and praying that it hadn't sunk. There was another silence. "Well?" I urged. "Do you know?"

I heard mom take a sharp intake of breath. "April of 1912," she said.

My heart sank. I had changed *nothing*, even though I gave E. J. Smith the irrefutable proof he'd asked for. I nodded to myself reluctantly, knowing my mom would know because she's a quiz whiz. Now there was another sharp intake of breath on the other end of the line.

"It sank in three hundred feet of water in New York harbour, after a raging fire in the boiler room caused a massive explosion, killing forty crew members and ten passengers," she announced matter-of-factly. "It was said to be an uneventful Atlantic crossing, except that the captain and his officers reported seeing a ghost on the evening of April 15th, which warned them of an impending collision with an iceberg."

Yippeeeeee! He had listened to me after all. They had listened to me. Fifty dead instead of fourteen hundred!

***

NOT FAR AWAY, in another time and another place, Terry and Frankie were planning another break-in. Frankie's eyes were dark and remote as he listened to Terry's deep, resonant and carefully modulated voice. He sat up straight in his chair, eyes wide, mouth hanging open.

"...It's worth thousands, so it's worth nickin'," Terry announced in a whisper. "We'll be able to fence it for fifty grand minimum, easy!"

Frankie smiled. "Fifty grand for robbin' an old girl of her

necklace. Wow! Now that's worth a sleepless night!" he said loudly.

"Shush, don't cause a scene," whispered Terry.

The diners in the light, cheerfully decorated bar/restaurant were staring at them both, frozen in silent tableau with forks or spoons halfway to mouth.

"Don't shush me! I haven't done anythin' wrong!" said Frankie.

Just then the waiter walked up to them and took their drinks order. Terry ordered a large vodka and Frankie ordered a double whisky. The waiter disappeared, returning moments later with their drinks and Frankie paid with a ten pound note; counting every penny of change he was given. He didn't tip the waiter either, with his hand held out expectantly, he just sneered and glared at him.

Oh, by the way, I was in my spectral form, watching and listening to every word they uttered. I had been keeping surveillance on them for several hours and didn't know whether it would help me, but I figured it couldn't hurt. Besides, I had acquired a morbid curiosity about the pair and wanted to know details of their everyday existence. I wanted to know what made them tick.

Terry's hand suddenly shot out and grabbed Frankie's hand in a vice like grip and he squeezed hard. "Listen you dumb twat, I'm trying to organise a fuckin' burglary and you're advertisin' it! When I say *Shush*, I expect you to shut the fuck up! *Got it?*"

Frankie's face was still, remote and completely controlled, showing no pain. "I've fuckin' got it, so you can let go of my hand now!" he snarled.

Terry squeezed harder. "You think you're as tough as an iron nail, don't you, you dumb fuck? Well I'll tell you this; I *am* harder than an iron nail, so cross me at your own peril.

You would still be rottin' in jail if it wasn't for me!"

The one thing Frankie would never do was dispute the fact that Terry *was* harder than an iron nail. In prison, Parkhurst to be exact, he had seen him drive a six-inch nail into a wooden fence post with just his fist. I'd seen him do it too!

I laughed inwardly. Then I had the strangest feeling, as if I was being watched and studied. I shivered at the thought, remembering a passage from a book I'd read called "Jumper", in which an eighteen year old man discovers he can teleport to anywhere in the world, simply by thinking about it. In the book he wondered if there were others who could do the same, and now I was wondering, what if there *are* other Time Travellers – dangerous ones? I thought about the night I leapt back to Fat Jack's bar to try and change things, the night I got knocked from my feet in the ally when the exit door swung open and hit me. I would have sworn I saw something huge, made of metal, glinting in the shadows behind me, its glaring red eyes staring at me. I shivered again. Or was it just my imagination running wild?

I thought of the opening lines from Ted Hughes' novel, "The Iron Giant". *The Iron Man came to the top of the cliff. How far had he walked? Nobody knows! Where had he come from? Nobody knows!* Maybe there are other Time Travellers! Maybe they are watching me!

I was sitting directly in front of Frankie and he stared right through me, blankly. There was a mirror on the wall by his side, reflecting his image, but not mine, and it was a strange feeling knowing that no one could see or feel me. In that single moment I thought about Jane again and her murder, of those shocking hours she must have endured at the hands of the monster sitting in front of me. *It was him. I know it was.* My mind dizzied and my knees suddenly threatened to give way. My stomach hurt, making it hard to breathe and I lashed out in anger at Frankie's face, two or three times with open-handed slaps, gritting my teeth. His head didn't move of course. How could it? I wasn't there in my physical form. My heart was pounding though, just the same, and I was having trouble catching my breath.

I had another thought. What if "National Security" somehow knows of my existence and my time-travelling capability? Would I be perceived as a threat – one to be removed somehow? I could imagine the fateful phone call...

"Mr. Ward, don't hang up, this is the head of M I 5."

"What do you want?"

"We want to know how you do what you do. We want you to work for *us!*"

"No, sorry, not interested."

"Then we'll have to delete you! We know where you are and can do it as easily as deleting a file on our computers!"

The word *delete* seems harmless enough, until you look up its synonyms. Erase! Rub out! Obliterate! Those three words alone conjured up enough scary images in my mind. Even worse – what if the other side knows about me and wants me to work for them. The KGB doesn't stand for *Killing, Guts and Blood,* but it might as well do. I could imagine a similar threatening phone call from them.

My mind snapped back from my reverie. Terry and Frankie were still arguing heatedly.

"You've caused me loads of fuckin' grief over the years, but I've always stood by you through thick and thin, so do me a big favour – shut the fuck up and open you ears instead!" Terry snapped, and his tone of voice reminded me of my dad when he used to chastise me as a kid, but without the expletives.

Frankie sat bolt upright, shocked and speechless for a fleeting moment. "Fuck you!" he snapped back angrily, furiously. It made both Terry and me jump, besides the rest of the patrons. Suddenly, there was silence in the bar/restaurant, spoons and forks frozen half way to mouths again on shocked, staring faces.

Frankie stood up, kicking his chair away with a clatter, pulling a knife on Terry. "The last cunt who spoke to me like that got his throat slit from ear to ear." He gestured it with the forefinger of his other hand.

Terry stared at the knife, eyes wide, hesitating for a moment, and then there was a click from under the table, sounding like a pistol being cocked. Terry's face hardened. "Never pull a knife on a man with a gun," he whispered, his lips hardly moving. "Now pick up the chair and sit the fuck down before I do something *you'll* regret! You're the only dumb fuck I know who would bring a knife to a gunfight!"

"*Jesus,* you'd shoot your best friend?" said Frankie nervously.

Terry grinned, lifting his hand out from under the table, flicking open an old Ronson lighter with a noisy click. Lighting a cigarette, he laughed good humouredly. "Yeah, I'd shoot. But only after my best friend became my worst enemy. Now for Christ's sake, pick up your chair and sit back down before I give you a slap!"

Frankie picked up the chair and sat back down. "Jesus, Terry, you had me cold there for a moment and almost scared the shite outta me! Thought that lighter was a goddam gun!" His body was charged with nervous energy and he was actually tingling.

Satisfied that Frankie posed no immediate threat, Terry relaxed a little. "You still havin' painful migraines and wild nightmares?"

The patrons of the café settled back down, not daring to venture their gaze in the direction of the two men again.

"Yeah," Frankie nodded. "The drugs don't help anymore. Even the higher doses don't work."

"Have you been to see the specialist that the doc referred you to?"

"Hell, no. I ain't lettin' some part-time butcher poke around inside my head," Frankie mused with a lopsided grin.

"Just wondered, because you seem more irritable and bad tempered these days. Your behaviour is quite bizarre and unpredictable. *Cranky* is a good word for it!'

"Need more sleep than I'm getting. The migraines keep me awake at night, and when I finally fall asleep the nightmares wake me up with a start, cold and shivering," groaned Frankie. He spun his head to look out of the cafe window, but his eyes didn't see the town square. Instead, he saw his drunken, abusive father snaking his belt out of his pants' loops, swinging it back and forth, striking him with the silver buckle winking in the dim light just before dawn. *How many times did you have to hit me dad? How many? And how many is too many?*

He flinched and blinked hard, the scene changing. His dad loomed over him at his mother's graveside. "It's your fault she's dead!" he was screaming. "She died giving birth to you, you ungrateful little shit!" The belt came out and the buckle hit again and again. *I'm sorry. I'm sorry. I'm sorry. I didn't want her to die. I didn't want to hurt her or you!*

Frankie flinched and shuddered, returning his gaze to Terry. "Guess I'll sleep enough when I'm dead and buried," he said, grateful to be out of the awful daydream.

For myself, I had seen and heard enough for one day, so I leapt back to the cabin in Scotland and poured a scotch with a splash of soda water. I walked to the front door for the freshly delivered newspaper. The Stirling *Herald* was in its infancy, but its circulation was growing rapidly. Stooping, I snatched it up and a supplement slipped out, fluttering to my feet. Picking that up too, I plodded wearily back to the living room, sitting back down on the couch, whisky in one hand, paper and supplement in the other.

Big, bold, blood-red letters on the front of the supplement asked: "What really happened to Jack the Ripper? Did he die or disappear?"

I was intrigued by the headline. I knew very little about the Ripper case, other than he was doing his evil work in the latter half of the year 1888, and that "Jack the Ripper" was a pseudonym given to an unidentified serial killer, active in the largely impoverished Whitechapel area and surrounding districts of London. The name originated in a letter sent to the media, namely the London Central News Agency by someone claiming to be the *Ripper*, the victims being prostitutes who had their throats savagely slit and various organs gruesomely removed. The brutal killings persisted until 1891 when they suddenly stopped for some unknown reason. Had the Ripper died, moved elsewhere, or been incarcerated in prison for lesser crimes? No one of that time knew, and I found the fact that he had killed five plus victims and was never caught quite astonishing.

I opened the supplement and read on. It stated many facts, even giving the location of murder sites – Osborn Street, George Yard, Durward Street, Hanbury Street, Berner Street, Mitre Square and Dorset Street – and I thought, *for something this well documented, why wasn't the Ripper ever identified?*

I read on again, and the article stated that the police investigation started on the 3rd of April 1888 and went on until the 13th February of 1891 – encompassing eleven separate killings in total, known on the police docket as the "Whitechapel Murders". And among the eleven murders actively investigated by the police, five are almost universally agreed upon as the work of a single killer. *Jack the Ripper.*

I read the whole ten page supplement. I read it again. And again, until I knew the facts off by heart, even though it was a puzzling, uncomfortable, intimidating and gruesome read. How the article described the mutilations and eviscerations of the women's fragile bodies made me want to puke, it was so gratuitously graphic. *Unfortunately, that's what sells newspapers. And always will!*

Standing up, I wandered over to the drinks bar, pouring myself another scotch, catching my reflection in the mirror. My expression was inscrutably morose, but why was that such a surprise after reading the Ripper article? I felt physically sick and depressed, finding myself mumbling a few words, shaking my head and chewing steadily on my thumbnail. Then it was decided, just like that. And I do mean – just like *that*.

I was now beginning to harbour a fascination for death. *Motive and means.* It was becoming an unhealthy fascination – and I knew it, but I couldn't seem to stop myself. It was definitely not right, but it didn't seem wrong either, and Jack the Ripper intrigued me in a dark macabre way, particularly as he had literally got away with murder several times, and then vanished like the night heat without a trace. I had made up my mind. My next destination in time was going to be 1888. And knowing the Ripper's killing pattern and locations, I was sure I could follow him in my spectral form and discover his identity – maybe even change into my physical form at some point to capture him and hand him over to the law. As usual the possibilities were endless – as is *Time*.

The site of the first killing, Durward Street, was going to be my primary destination. Mary Ann Nichols (nicknamed Polly by her friends) was murdered on Friday 31st August 1888. Her body was discovered by market porter, Charles Cross, at about 6:40am, on the ground in front of a gated stable entrance in Buck's Row – now Durward Street – a back street, two hundred yards from the London Hospital. Her throat had been severed so deeply by two cuts that she was almost decapitated, and the lower part of her abdomen was ripped open by a deep jagged wound. There were also several deep incisions across the abdomen.

I glanced at the Grandfather clock, listening to its steady regular tick. The time was 2:00pm. I marched purposefully into the bedroom and changed my clothes, finally slipping on a dark overcoat, and I picked up the Time Machine from the dresser drawer, switching it on. Once again there seemed to be a breath of wind in the cabin and the lights dimmed. It began to buzz. "Verbal commands only," I ordered when the mainframe screen came up, having no idea what the Space-Time coordinates were that I needed to get to my destination. "Year: 1888. Date: 31st of August. Time: 5:30am. Place: Durward Street, London, England," I continued.

"Calculating!" the machine said in its familiar artificial voice. It vibrated in my hand, clicked several times and buzzed loudly as if gears were working overtime in thought. "Correction!" it suddenly blurted in a matter-of-fact tone. "Buck's Row (*now* renamed Durward Street) is your destination – confirm?" Once again it actually sounded irritated by my incompetence at not giving the exact information.

I glared at the screen. "Confirmed!" *Bloody know-it-all machine!* But it made me feel safe knowing it had established exactly what it was doing and where and when I was going. It scrolled to the third screen, buzzed even louder and off I went through the vast, seemingly endless, wormhole of Time.

Instantly my mind reeled in a kind of fog again, feeling the strange sensation of weightlessness – of flying. Suddenly, there was a blinding flash of light and the nauseating, sickly feeling stopped. I opened my eyes and everything was still spinning. It took a few moments to focus properly, but when I did, I realised I was standing in a dimly lit backstreet with a gas-lamp at either end.

With the moon behind a screen of clouds, mist swirled in murky trailers just above the ground, making the street look ghostly – eerie. I swallowed hard, glancing about nervously, suddenly remembering I had arrived here in my physical form instead as my spectral self. I felt very vulnerable and it made me even more nervous. Now my palms were cold and sweaty from being clenched tightly.

The street was quiet and seemed deserted, except for a tramp slouched in the recesses of a nearby doorway. He had jumped with a start when I appeared by his side, but then he went back to sleep in his drunken stupor. A bitterly cold wind was blowing down the street and it was drizzling rain as I glanced down at the face of the Time Machine. It glowed in the dark, announcing that I had arrived at my requested destination, and the time was exactly 5:30 am.

My mind drifted back to the article in the supplement: *at about 11:00 pm. on the 30th of August, Nichols was seen walking the Whitechapel Road; at 1:30 am, she was seen to leave a pub in Brick Lane, Spitalfields. An hour later, she left her common lodging-house in Thrawl Street as she hadn't enough money to bed down for the night. She was last spotted at the corner of Osborn Street and the Whitechapel Road, wearing her newly acquired bonnet at about 5:30 am., an hour before her death. At 6:40 am, she was found dead on the street where I was now standing.*

The new moon slid behind another curtain of clouds as I lurched up the street tentatively in the dark, looking for the all-important spot where Nichols would be found dead by the porter, in front of the gated stable entrance. Suddenly a black cat shot out of the shadows, scaring me half to death. My heart raced and pounded and my body shook as I watched it run up the street and disappear around the corner.

The air was still and I was alone. I moved on up the street slowly, my back to the walls of the house fronts, and a patch of moonlight came through the clouds illuminating the whole street for a moment. Then it was dark again. Mist drifted and stirred about my knees and I couldn't see my shoes. However, I was almost sure that I could hear faint footsteps behind me, quickening, getting closer and closer.

Suddenly, the footsteps stopped. I turned. A tall, broad man darted forward from out of the shadows with a needle sharp dagger, the blade glinting in the dim light of the street lamp as he thrust it up under my chin, pricking the skin, drawing blood.

I'm a dead man! The Ripper is going to cut my throat before he does away with Nichols, I thought.

My assailant pushed his meaty face nose-to-nose with mine, his black eyes wide; his mad gaze unblinking. He smiled a lop-sided, toothless smile, cutting my skin deeper. His breath burned against my skin fetid and raw. "What – what do you want?" I stammered; my voice a whisper, my throat bone dry.

"Give me some money or I'll cut your throat!" was the reply. He pricked the blade deeper still, lifting me to my toes. I could feel warm blood trickling down my neck and I was shaking like a leaf, but paralysed with fear.

"How much do you want?" I asked. Fear must have been shining in my eyes.

"How much have you got?"

"Very little..."

"Then hand over what you have and I'll let you live," my assailant wheezed.

With the knife still at my throat, I began to turn out my

pockets and his eyes shone when he noticed the few silver coins in my right hand. But they shone brighter still when he noticed the metallic glint of the Time Machine in my left hand. He snatched it from me, dropping it in the process. It clattered to the cobbled street and he knelt to try and pick it up, keeping the knife blade pointing at me.

I had to do something. Something *desperate*. Or I would be dead in the next few moments. Just then, my attacker reached for the shiny machine, fingers stretching, trying to pick it up. Moving his eyes away from me momentarily, he looked at the machine. It was then I grabbed the wrist of his knife hand and punched him hard in the face. He dropped the knife, but clung onto the machine as I tried to take it away from him. We began to struggle. Wrestle. I punched him in the face again, but he didn't let go of me or the machine. Then he must have accidently switched the machine on, because I heard it buzz in his hand. "Where to, Time Traveller?" it asked.

Without even thinking, I said, "Take me and this *scumbag* to the future, to the last day of the Earth's life – do it now!" *This was my only hope for survival...*

The Time Machine buzzed, vibrating louder, its gears and mechanisms working overtime. Instantly, I was overcome by the familiar feeling of weightlessness and felt incredibly nauseous as everything around me spun wildly. Then there was a flash of light and we were there – thirty million years hence. I was stunned by what I saw. Eddying flakes of snow were dancing before my eyes, blown on a moaning wind and the Earth was now no more than an ice ball, while our sun was in its final death throws. I watched it swelling into a red giant, engulfing Mercury, then Venus, the darkness around us growing apace. We had literally seconds to live as the sun carried on engulfing our solar system and my attacker's eyes were wide, shining with terror, not understanding the situation. To him, it was like a dreadful dream, not at all familiar.

I swallowed hard, my throat so dry and tight that it actually hurt. I wasn't imagining this. It *was* real. It was happening *now!* And I probably had less than five seconds to live. But there was tiredness in my muscles after fighting my adversary for the Time Machine. *The Time Machine! Where is it?* I took a large breath and then another. My eyes searched. It was still in *his* hand! I snatched it from my attacker as the sun's huge shape threatened to engulf the earth. "Verbal command – take me home, now!" I screamed with every ounce of strength I had left.

Chapter 12
STIRLING. SCOTLAND. PRESENT DAY.

I had blacked out to the sound of my attacker's dreadful screams as I leapt back through the centuries, and I woke up on the floor in the cabin in Scotland, knowing exactly where I was even before I opened my eyes, due to the steady tick of the Grandfather clock and the smell of heather outside.

What had happened to me seemed to be no more than a nightmarish dream now. I stood up, glancing at my reflection in the mirror and not surprisingly, I looked much worse than the last time I saw myself. Staring at the Grandfather clock, I noted the time. It was one minute past two in the afternoon. I had been gone for only sixty seconds, yet I had what looked to be at least a day's growth of stubble on my chin, a desperate gleam in my eyes and an air of nervous tension hung over me because of what had just happened.

Picking up the supplement, I stared at it. Nothing about the Ripper article had changed and it would have, had my attacker been him. So who was he? Was he just a common low-life? A scumbag after my small change? Whose ass had I actually dumped in the future to die? I had no idea, but did know he would have slit my throat without a second thought, just to get his hands on some money and my shiny machine. So, I felt no remorse whatsoever for what I had done. *Do unto those who would do unto you. Only do it first!*

Strangely, somehow I felt like a comic book superhero championing a cause, protecting the people of Earth, and that history would vindicate me for my judgment and unethical actions in this one particular matter. It was after all, him or me and somehow, somewhere I had become a man of vision who understands the hard decisions and sacrifices necessary to make this world a better place. And if the laws of the land are inadequate and judges cannot dish out the justice needed, then I could and would, because as a practicing lawyer I saw the Justice System fail, time after time.

Suddenly, I realised that I hadn't eaten for hours and was starving hungry, so I went to the kitchen and cooked fried bacon, eggs and tomatoes with toast and coffee, and rammed it down my throat as quickly as I could without stopping to burp even. I regretted it later. The indigestion was almost more than I could bear. Then, I seemed to blink and it was almost 10:00 pm. *How time flies.* I decided to have an early night and headed for bed, taking the Time Machine with me. Placing it back in the dresser drawer, I locked it, pocketing the key. *What new adventures await me tomorrow,* I wondered? Turning out the light, I was asleep the instant my head touched the pillow. *Good night and God bless Jane.*

***

SOMEWHERE SECRET IN NORFOLK, Sir Jeremy Collins-Smyth, his manner sullen, spoke in a low nasal voice. Dressed in a Harris Tweed suit and tweed hat, he paced the front of the top security facility aided by a walking stick. His hair was jet black and he sported a pencil thin mustache. "What the hell happened here?" he asked, his eyes scanning the wrecked facility for any signs of life. There was none. The place had been levelled to the ground by some dread force and everything was blackened. Charred. Smouldering. And trailers of smoke and ash drifted on the light breeze.

The two, 5 star generals by his side shook their heads solemnly, not knowing what to say. Then a voice came over their hand-held radio and someone cleared their throat at the other end. "...Goddam it all to hell, I've checked everything! Every last one of the CCTV tapes and there's nothing on them, other than flickering black and white images and static instead of sound!" The radio clicked off and fell silent.

"So, we have no clue as to what happened here and no idea where the robot is. We just have piles of dust instead of guards!" said one of the generals.

The second general nodded. "I did say at the time; don't send lambs to guard a lion. The Military should have been given this responsibility, not bloody ex-Securicor guards. It was sheer madness and asking for trouble!"

This time, Smyth, shook his head and then nodded, not knowing what to think or say. He paced up and down the ruined facility impatiently, prodding the rubble and ash for clues as to what might have happened.

A thoughtful observer, made completely of an unknown metal alloy, standing hidden, not so very far away noticed Smyth nodding and then shaking his head in dismay. Then the observer disappeared.

***

IN THE NOT SO DISTANT PAST, Terry and Frankie were arguing again.

"...Are you fuckin' brain dead, or do you aspire to be an ignorant asshole? Or is that just my perception of you?" Terry snapped. "*GODDAM IT*, do I have to do everything myself? Jesus, you're fuckin' hopeless and I can't trust you to do a single thing right!"

Frankie smiled a lopsided grin, waiting for the never-ending tirade of abuse to cease. "Don't mince your words, you fuck. Say what you really think for a change!" Frankie snapped back finally in a high pitched tone. "It doesn't matter what I do for you, it's never fuckin' good enough! You always find fault!"

Pointedly, Terry looked at his watch, pulling the parking notice from behind the wiper blade of their car. He crumpled it up, noticing the wheel clamp. "For fuck's sake, Frankie, I've only been gone ten minutes, so where were you while they were clamping this piece of shite?"

"Had to take a leak! Nature called!"

"Well, Nature didn't call at all when they were handin' out *brains,* you dumb twat. This is supposed to be a getaway. I've just robbed an old lady's jewellery shop around the corner, *remember.* That's what we came for, *right?!*" barked Terry.

"Yeah," Frankie agreed, zipping his fly.

"I'm beginning to feel like I'm in a fuckin' Laurel and Hardy movie, because it could only happen to me!"

Suddenly police sirens were heard in the distance, getting closer by the second.

Terry stared at the wheel clamp and then at Frankie. "We need to get out of here quick! And I do mean now!"

Frankie nodded dumbly. Then, in an unbelievable twist of fate, a double-decker bus rumbled around the corner and Frankie stuck his hand out immediately without even thinking. The bus pulled over to the curb and stopped. Both men jumped on board, staring back at their car by the bus stop, and the bell rang as the bus took off speedily down the main street, with Frankie and Terry staring at the passing police cars racing to the scene of the robbery.

"You're a dumb shit, but a lucky one," said Terry breathing a sigh of relief. "I didn't notice it was a bus stop until the bus came."

"Me neither," Frankie admitted. "No wonder they clamped the car while I was having a piss."

The scowl disappeared from Terry's face and both men laughed.

***

THE NEXT MORNING, in Scotland, in the present day it was beginning to rain. I was still exhausted and my eyes were heavy, however, even though I still felt sleepy, really sleepy, I had decided to take a long walk to clear my head of cobwebs, not thinking at all about the weather. The path I was taking was covered with moss and lichen and was through thick undergrowth, mixed with ferns and thorny vines that kept scratching my bare legs. The surrounding trees were thick, spaced far apart and beneath their filigree canopy it was cool and dark, and from moment to moment the scent of the forest mixed with the rain intoxicated me, making me feel quite light headed.

Suddenly, there was a flash of lightning. Seconds later thunder drummed out overhead, but I didn't mind as I've never been afraid of either, and love walking in the rain. It felt great. I was feeling great too. Better than I had for a long time. My old hurtful wounds were finally healing. However, I was beginning to think that I was carrying my fascination for time travel, death and the past to the point of obsession. Yet, how could I not? I had acquired something that would alter anyone's life forever, the gift of a lifetime. No, the gift of ages!

"Today is the Tomorrow we worried about Yesterday..." is a quote I didn't understand when I first heard a friend say it at my wife's funeral. I understand it now though, because I can visit yesterday or tomorrow at will and return to today. Although, I don't think my friend's interpretation of that quote is what he had in mind at the time he spoke the words, quite frankly.

Now as I rambled on through the forest, I considered the future of the human race. I knew exactly how it was going to end – thirty million years hence – and that single thought alone was scary. Yet on the spin of the coin, I didn't know what was going to happen tomorrow or the next day. However, in the meanwhile, I could keep on trying to perform the miracle of changing certain parts of history for the greater good.

I also began asking myself a lot of questions. Such as: *what if I'm not really time-travelling? What if I'm actually flicking back and forth between parallel universes? Suppose for instance that there are an infinite number of parallel universes out there as Einstein and others have speculated, and each one is different in some way, with a small change that has altered its course over a period of time, like a pile of the same novel with each having a slight deviation in the storyline. What if, when I seem to be travelling in time, I'm actually hopping between these universes, following that slightly different path? Maybe the universe I leave carries on as it's supposed to and I hop between them at will, until I find my ideal universe, where my wife is still alive. Maybe I haven't changed history at all before. Maybe I've just swapped for the universe with the course I prefer!*

I tripped, coming back from my thoughts. It was dark now and I was beginning to stumble over the rutted ground. I pulled my torch from my deep coat pocket, switching it on, pointing the beam at my feet to see what I'd tripped over. It was just a length of tree root. Raising the torch, a ghostly white face screamed at me out of the blackness, scaring me half to death, and I barked in surprise like a startled sea-lion.

"Where the hell did you come from?" asked the small female in a whisper.

"Where the hell did *you* come from? Scared the living daylights out of me! Jesus, I nearly had a heart attack right there and then!" I said, clutching my chest.

"I was out rambling and got a little lost!"

"Lady, there isn't such a thing as being a little lost. Either you *are* or you're not, and that's a fact. And to be honest, I think *I'm* lost too." I stared at her face in the torchlight, laughing in relief as she was no savage alien, come to Earth just to kill me for my time-travelling antics.

I remembered my manners. "Sorry if I scared you."

She didn't answer me straight away. She just gave me an

odd look. Maybe she thought *I* was an alien from the planet Ratatouille.

"*Great!*" she said finally. "*We're both lost!* I can look after myself, but I hate the dark. Always have, right from being a tiny tot."

"I'm scared of the dark too!" said I.

She looked at me oddly again. "A big guy like you shouldn't be scared of the dark. You're kidding me, right?" She smiled.

"Yeah, I'm kidding..."

Suddenly a soft yellow glow bathed the both of us. It was car headlights. Then, I heard the screeching of tyres and realised we were probably no more than fifty feet away from the main highway. Turning off the torch, I put it back in my pocket and could see the car through the trees. The driver's door was open and he was standing taking a pee in the headlights. I squinted against the light, waiting until he'd finished and then shouted at him. "Hello there!"

The man jumped. "What the bloody hell...?" he said, sounding annoyed, zipping his fly.

I quickly glanced over my shoulder at the woman. She had obviously seen the man taking a leak and averted her eyes momentarily, but her face coloured bright red with embarrassment in the dim light. Leading the way to the car, I stopped in front of the driver and he looked at me, then at the woman.

"Yer startled me!" he said, looking like a rabbit caught in the headlights. Fidgeting nervously, he checked his fly to make sure it was zipped. It *was*.

"Looks like we've all had a bit of a fright tonight then," said the woman, wiping the rain from her face.

The man splashed around the car to the driver's side, gritting his teeth. He jumped in. "Bloody scared me half to death, yer did, the pair of yer. Miles from anywhere in the dark and you come boundin' out the woods at me!"

I grinned. "Sorry friend. Didn't mean to startle you, but we're lost. Could you give us a lift back to town?"

The driver scowled. "Let's get somethin' straight! I ain't yer friend and I don't give strangers a lift!" With that he fired up the engine and zoomed off into the distance, leaving me feeling rather silly, besides being cold and wet.

Turning to face the woman, I opened my mouth, but stopped the words when I saw her face.

"Didn't think he'd just leave us out here," she said, looking aghast.

I half smiled. "At least you're not alone!"

She gave me a weak smile and sighed. "Yeah, right, and you're lost too – remember."

I shrugged. "Maybe another car will come along soon."

She laughed grimly, mirthlessly. "Yeah, and they'll probably leave us out here in the dark too. I hate the dark!" Grumpily, she stamped her feet in a puddle like a naughty little girl.

"Cheer up," I said; trying to think of a plan of action, "at least we're out here on the main road, not still lost in that dark wood."

"Yeah, some careless driver will probably run us over out here," she said gloomily.

I shook my head. "Lady, you're just a bundle of joy to be around. I only met you five minutes ago and you've depressed the hell out of me already!"

She stared at me. "Well, pardon me for being scared of the dark!"

I remembered my manners again and shrugged. "Sorry, but no one has ever died of the dark!"

She stared at me again, harder, and began to laugh. "That's

funny."

"Ah, finally a smile," said I. "You had me worried, I thought you'd had it surgically removed."

She laughed harder. "I'm sorry for being a *scaredy-cat!*"

Suddenly, a cold chill ripped through me like an electric shock. Either my imagination was running wild and my eyes playing tricks on me, or there was something huge, made of metal glinting in the shadows of the forest, its glaring red eyes staring at the pair of us laughing. I shivered and turned to look at the woman.

"What's wrong?" she asked.

I must have looked to be in a daze, a stupor, staring back into the shadows of the forest. If there had been something there it was gone now, or so I thought. The woman put her hand into her bag and began pulling something out. Suddenly, there was an intense flash of blinding red light. I winced, blinking hard, my body feeling very heavy and as if my clothes were red hot, shrinking about me. The woman vaporised before my eyes, leaving nothing but a wisp of smoke and a pile of dirty grey ash at my feet. I shivered. Horrified. Blinking, I closed my eyes and opened them again.

Now, I was standing in bright sunlight, the air about me warm but damp, and birds chirruped in the surrounding trees. I had a massive headache and was in shock. *What just happened? What the hell's going on*, I thought. *One minute I'm out in the dark and it's raining, and the next minute I'm stood in bright daylight.* I was standing on a narrow path, near what looked like mud huts with plumes of black smoke rising from thatched roofs. Shafts of sunlight penetrated the thick foliage above my head, dappling the ground and I could smell something wonderful wafting my way on the breeze.

I breathed the air deeply. My body was stiff and felt like I'd been hit by a train and my headache was getting worse.

Have I imagined what I think just happened? Am I going mad, I thought? Yet I sensed somehow that the Time Machine was the key to everything that was happening. *Was I somehow slipping between parallel universes without even knowing? Or does time fluctuate of its own accord?* The answers to all of these questions eluded me entirely.

I took out my watch. It was 10:00 am, and the sun glared in my eyes. *Where the hell am I?* I sensed I was still in Scotland because the scenery was familiar, but I had the distinct feeling that I wasn't in the present day. And if this were true, how could it be, as I hadn't used the Time Machine.

Panic crept through me. *What the hell is going on?* I forced myself to remain calm. There was a logical explanation for all of this, I reasoned, but didn't know what it was. I glanced about more carefully this time. Something wasn't right. I placed my hand into my deep coat pocket and pulled out the machine, turning it on. There was a beep, then the familiar buzzing sound. Scrolling the screens to the Space-Time Coordinates, I stared at them, swallowing hard and couldn't believe my eyes. It read: Scotland, 1216 A.D.

An arrow suddenly struck me in the left shoulder, the steel point punching through to the other side, the impact knocking me to my knees. Staggered, I winced, gasping for breath, trying to fill my lungs and I cursed not knowing what was happening, but I managed to climb to my feet. Instantly, I was knocked back to the ground by an old man wearing a brown robe. "What are you doing wandering about out here?" the man gasped, pushing me down into the dirt as an arrow struck him full in the chest, and another passed through his throat. Making a feeble effort to rise, he looked surprised and coughed blood, falling back into a seated position, stone cold dead.

"*Jesus*," I found myself saying, surprised by the suddenness of the attack.

There was a bright flash of light and I was surrounded by several men on horseback, the riders wearing suits of armour and black plumed helms. Their horses were draped in red cloth, studded with silver and the men looked ominous. The leader reared his horse repeatedly and it stomped the ground with its forelegs, missing me by mere inches.

The mystery deepened. *How did I get here?*

Moments earlier, when I had looked at the Time Machine's screen, it had said: Scotland, 1216 A.D., yet I had not programmed it for this place or time, so what had happened? *I truly believe I am going mad!*

"You're a poacher on the king's land!" a voice announced.

Despite the cool air I was sweating profusely, anxious and afraid, my skin cold, my heart pounding. And listening to the rider's voice, which was deep and harsh, did nothing to bolster my flagging courage. "I'm no poacher!" I replied.

"The penalty for poaching the king's land is a death sentence!" said the rider, drawing his sword. His voice was so loud that it rang in my ears. He raised the weapon high into the air and paused as if relishing the moment. Then the blade came slashing down. Blackness engulfed me once again.

Chapter 13
STIRLING. SCOTLAND. PRESENT DAY.

I awoke with a start, drenched in sweat, my heart beating like a hammer in my chest. I'd fallen asleep in my easy chair before going for my long walk and dreamt the whole thing, thank God!

Now I think about time constantly, imagining the impossible happening, but I've realised that I'm driven by choice and not instinct. I do what I want, when I want. However, is it possible that we're hardwired to *Time* without even knowing it? I decided to try something strange – something unorthodox. I wouldn't wear a watch for the rest of my stay in Scotland. I know, it doesn't like a groundbreaking experiment, but I needed some answers and this was a beginning, a place to start.

So, I isolated myself in my own world of time, reporting only to my diary, deciding to let my body wake when it wanted to, eat, pee, poo, exercise and fall asleep when it wanted to, and see if I lost track of time. Would I know by this method whether I'd slept one hour or ten? I found out after a period of only one week. Even though I lost track of time in my mind, a pattern emerged as I still followed my usual cycle of sleeping, waking and other bodily functions. Astonishingly, I realised that something was controlling my timing from within, and deduced from this that a human being has an internal body-clock, which is completely independent from *Mother Earth's* cycle, thus proving that I'm a slave to my own body-clock.

Time, it seems, is a biological mechanism controlling our behaviour, besides the universe, so I decided to test myself even further, apart from the sleep, wake cycle and human functions. Now I was looking for the effects of time in everything, even down to the cortisol in my stress hormones and my muscle strength, discovering that throughout a normal day, my physical performance changes dramatically, due to the effects of time. I know that even the chemicals in my saliva are subject to time's influence, and know this, thanks to a stack of library books with unpaid dues. So after a whole week of reading and testing, I found out just what was going on.

It turns out that almost all of our bodily processes follow very predictable cycles that are controlled by time, and one master clock that orchestrates every fibre of our being – an organ, which is a cluster of only twenty thousand cells and no bigger than a pea, deep within our brains, called the *Suprachiasmatic Nucleus* synchronises everything. I couldn't stop reading.

Now, *Time* for me has become an external pressure, a force of speed and punctuality that moves into all aspects of my life – work and personal. And it's terrifying to realise that from dawn to dusk, I'm driven by it as it relentlessly ticks off the seconds and minutes of my life. Subsequently, I've found myself timing everything without even noticing it – the boiling of a kettle, the changing of traffic lights and even the timing of a bad joke. Is this an innate sixth sense we all possess? If not, how do we all do this?

I was and still am fascinated. What about time and the universe? Has that got an all-powerful, all knowing clock too? Is *reality* a fabric? Are there really parallel universes, wormholes or multiverses? If so, are there real consequences with the implications?

This leads nicely back to Einstein's unpublished theories of Quantum Physics. In his lifetime, did he only touch the tip of the iceberg with his calculations and studies, or did he actually manage to combine all of the ingredients to conquer and master them, creating my Time Machine? Would I ever know the answers, I pondered, hauling myself to my feet. I walked over to the bar, pouring myself a scotch with a splash of water, studying my every action, which took a second here or two seconds there. *They all eventually add up to a whole lifetime,* I thought. I walked to the bedroom, counting my steps, each one denoting an increment of time. Opening my dresser drawer I stared at the shiny machine, which had somehow hijacked my life. And I blessed the day it had!

***

NOT VERY FAR AWAY, in another time, Terry and Frankie were sitting planning their next robbery.

"...For fuck's sake Frankie, will you stop pickin' your nose and listen to me! I'm beginning to think you're the stupid person's idea of a clever person, and you believe it yourself. What bit of brain you do possess is gonna fall out through that black hole your finger is jammed up, and it'll happen one day soon because you're a fuckin' walkin' almanac of self-abuse and affront, lookin' to demolish someone most of the time when they upset you. Can't you get through a day without slappin' or stabbin' somebody?" Terry pushed his meaty face nose to nose with Frankie's. His hard set eyes were wide.

Frankie ignored Terry's tirade of abuse, turning his head casually to stare out at the grey day, seemingly in deep thought – unfamiliar territory – while puffing on a cigarette. "I like inflicting pain. I'm good at it!" he sniped. "I can be inexhaustible and endlessly inventive!"

Terry nodded. "Yeah, but your small mind usually has the flexibility of a fuckin' telegraph pole, and there's less in your head than meets the eye!" Terry snapped back. "You missed the point of our last conversation on this subject and you're missing the point now. When we're doin' a caper, we need to keep a low profile to stay under the police radar, not fuckin' advertise it in the local newspaper – you *idiot!* If brains were gunpowder, you wouldn't have enough to blow your hat off!"

Frankie shook his head. "I ain't got a hat!" he sniped back dumbly, looking mean and moody.

"There you go again, missing the point. I'm sure there's a village somewhere, missing an idiot!" spat Terry looking angry and frustrated. "You're the only man I know who could start a fight in an empty room. Do you take an instant dislike to everyone you meet, just to save time? You seem to think you're charming, intelligent and witty, when you're really obnoxious and solemn with delusions of grandeur!"

Frankie nodded, then shook his head, then nodded, not knowing what to make of Terry's harsh comments. Then came the shouting and arguing that was loud enough to hear in the next universe.

Terry looked around the whitewashed basement, which contained mechanisms for sexual depravity, torture and abuse beyond his imagination, and he shook his head, anger pouring through his mind. "I know this is a stupid question," he suddenly said, "but how the fuck do you sleep at night?"

Frankie closed his eyes so he didn't have to look at Terry. Spit was dribbling from the side of his mouth as he imagined his last young female victim in the basement. He had heard himself say, *"You fuckin' love it!"* And he visualised himself ripping into the girl, yelling and laughing. She had pleaded for her life and then turned angry when he wouldn't let her go. She had shouted and screamed. "You fuckin' animal, can't you get a girlfriend? Is your dick too small?" Then she had prayed to God.

He pictured himself stuffing her lace panties into her mouth to shut her up. She had spit them out. "Let me go, you deranged bastard!" she had screamed with terror in her eyes. He had punched her with his clenched fist and she had gone limp and silent, so he had raped her again and then slit her throat, finally burying her in a corner of the basement where several more corpses were buried under lime to stop the awful stench.

He loved the horror of it all. The sheer terror his victims must feel knowing they're going to die and they can't stop it happening. What power he felt. He opened his eyes again. "Did I ever tell you that my father was a cop? He did everything by the book, believed in the law, wanted me to be a solicitor, drank in moderation, didn't smoke and paid his life insurance premiums on time. Then he died of a massive heart attack, aged fifty four, leaving me to fend for myself at the age of six years old. So tell me, where's the fuckin' logic or justice in that?"

Terry stared at him. "Your point is?"

Frankie laughed, "Always live for today. Tomorrow might not *come!*"

Terry shook his head. "You just love hurtin' people, one way or another. Either you break their bones and make their arms and legs bend both ways, or you chop pieces off them just to hear them scream. Well, let me ask you somethin' you moron. Did I make a big mistake when I partnered up with you? I recently told you we could steal fifty thousand pounds, and then I showed you *how* we could do it. And you still fuck up by gettin' the getaway car *clamped.* Don't think I can trust you anymore. If left to your own devices, you'd either be skinning someone alive or sitting on a bar-stool somewhere, penniless and drunk, after you've fucked everything that moves!"

Frankie shrugged. "Way of the world. I always wanted to be a dead hero like my father, not a live coward. I'm neither!"

"You won't ever be a hero, but you will be *wanted* alright. Dead or alive by the police. *Preferably dead!*" Terry snapped. "Heed my warning. The next time you go out to kidnap an innocence woman, armed police might be waitin' for you, because they must have put on extra patrols by now."

***

IN THE PRESENT DAY I stared solemnly at the Time Machine and turned it on, scrolling to the third screen. The E=MC2 equation stared me in the face, but what did the four tiny dials above it do? I decided to test them. Pensively, I hovered my finger over the first dial and could feel my heart racing and my face must have been pinched with anguish, but I pressed it and waited. Suddenly, the familiar voice of the machine announced, "Super-Electromagnet on, Time Traveller!"

There was the familiar breath of wind as the bedroom lamp dimmed and went out. Then there was almighty crashes from somewhere down the hallway; and to me it sounded to be coming from the kitchen. The light came back on. I swung around, catching my reflection in the mirror, indistinct and ghostlike as I walked out of the bedroom and down the hallway towards the kitchen. When I arrived I couldn't believe my eyes. Everything metallic – no matter what – was hovering near the ceiling or stuck to the walls. I blinked; my eyes wide and blinked again. Glancing down at the machine in my hand, its fluorescent face was lit up like a torch. I pressed the same dial again. There was another almighty crash as everything metal hit the floor. "Super-electromagnet off'," said the machine, matter-of-factly.

I stood silently, flabbergasted by what I'd seen. Marching back to the bedroom, I pressed the second dial. The machine's digital face glowed eerily. "Super-X-ray on!" it announced. At which point my reflection reappeared, looking like a skeleton in the mirror, and the bedroom wall became indistinct and ghostlike. Then *it* disappeared. I waited for a few moments and then reset the dial, the wall returning just as solid as ever.

I pressed the third dial. "Which gas do you require to be? Argon, Neon, Krypton or Xenon?" the machine asked. Just those few words created a climate of exciting possibilities. Neon was the only one I recognised and knew anything about, so that's what I said. Again, there was a breath of air, my lamp went out and I lit up like a ghostly illumination, my body crackling with static electricity as I moved around the room slowly.

I told the machine to cancel my order and I returned to my former self, staring at the forth dial. *What secrets lay beneath that final shiny face,* I thought? Quickly, without thinking and without caution, I pressed it and the machine whirred, its cogs and gears making a strange unfamiliar sound. "Matter transfer to energy," it said in a sort of muffled, but clipped tone. I gulped, sat down on the bed and went straight through it as if its molecules had rearranged themselves around my body. I jumped to my feet, fell forward and went straight through the bedroom wall into the hallway and began to sink down into the concrete floor as if it was quicksand. Hastily I pressed the forth dial again. "Energy transfer to matter," said the machine in the same clipped tone.

In a blur, the bed, wall and floor returned to normal, the molecules reforming like crystals in a kaleidoscope right before my eyes. I walked back up the hallway into the bedroom. *I don't believe what just happened! It was jaw- dropping! Mind-blowing! Bizarre even!* However, I had to admit to myself that I was mystified as to the possible use of the four dials, even though their function seemed to be quite awesome. *Maybe I'll find clues to it all later?* And so, over the next couple of days I pushed my exploration of the dials further, thinking that I had missed some subtle point that the machine was trying to make.

It was the morning of the third day when I finally realised

that the Time Machine was far more ingenious and far more complicated than I had first thought. Not only could I travel through the wormholes of *Time* in a solid form, but I could occupy any space, alter matter, change myself into an electro-magnet, become a gas or be an invisible spectre. I felt like a god and was staggered by the endless possibilities and properties of the tiny machine, the inventor of which must have been an absolute genius.

I had entered a Golden Age of pure discovery. An age like no other, and had now overcome my fear of the unknown. In fact, as far as the time-travelling was concerned, I'd become fearless to the point of being reckless as I look back upon those times now. And the Time Machine is, as far as I know, the first and only one of its kind, and the greatest modern instrument ever devised. How many ordinary people would sell their grandmothers, nay their whole family to get their hands on such an awesome device? So, why had fate picked me to be its owner – if indeed it had?

Now I deduced that *Space* and *Time* must be tunneled enormously somehow, and that these tunnellings were the entrances and exits through which I had been able to pass. My notion was definitely plausible and it was a theory that I assumed to be true. It was at this time that I made the most amazing discovery of all, when I visited my future-self in the year 2045 A.D. Come with me now and I'll explain it in great detail.

Chapter 14

My experiments with the Time Machine were now over. I had, I believed, discovered the inner workings of its artificial intelligence and was sure that there was no more to discover. However, I was wrong! Radically so! I found this out when I decided to visit my own life and times, forty years hence. I was in for the shock of my life and could never have guessed what I would discover.

I arrived in my spectral form in the blink of an eye, after ordering the Time Machine to take me thus far. A fire burned brightly in the room I was now occupying and a soft radiance filled it. It was a luxurious room, full of softly ticking clocks and it had an after-dinner ambiance with six men and six women sitting lazily, admiring the earnestness of the after-dinner speaker – who must have been in his eighties – and I didn't recognise him at first with his mop of curly white hair, goatee beard and mustache. But then I realised it was me. My future-self.

The twelve sitting guests were obviously from the media, the world's press to be exact, and each had a white badge clipped to their lapel, showing their photograph, besides a microphone in their hand. I listened to the ongoing conversation between them and my future-self, watching my dark eyes sparkle and shine and my face flush animatedly.

"…Is that not a rather large assumption for anyone to make, given the circumstances?" asked a reporter, cocking his head to one side thoughtfully.

In my spectral form I watched my other-self nod. "So it would seem. However, there is rather more to this story than meets the eye!"

"Do you really expect us to believe what you've just said?" a second male reporter asked.

"I don't expect you to believe anything without seeing the *proof!*" my alter-ego said. "Even I wouldn't believe such a thing without concrete evidence in my hands."

"You know that some of Einstein's mathematical theories and formulas were quite flawed, don't you?" said a female reporter.

"I've proved this one isn't!" said my future-self with a tone of conviction. "And I have the object in question in my possession that I proved it with, if anyone would like to see it. Its manufacture is now complete, finished last month."

"You have an actual prototype already built?" said the New York Times reporter looking stunned.

"I most certainly have," said my future-self, smiling like a Cheshire Cat.

Now *I* was curious. What was this press conference about? What had I made? I listened intently to an argumentative female reporter with auburn hair, expounding her own thoughts on the subject being debated. "Time has no real existence! It only came into being when clocks were invented and exists only in our minds."

"You Missy are undeniably and irrefutably wrong!" said my future-self. "Time *is* a real fabric, just as surely as Space is, and one cannot exist without the other. There are Black-Holes in space, and Time is riddled with Wormholes that can be traversed."

Another reporter of large proportions with dark hair and a wide mustache came to his feet, holding up his microphone. "This is all conjecture, none of which can be proved professor!" he announced in booming voice.

Good Lord, I'm a professor in the future, I thought, *but a professor of what?*

"You're not following me," said my future-self. "A Time Machine exists. I engineered it at Cal-Tech and it has specific features and functions. The Sat-Nav, or to give it its full title, the Sub-Atomic, Time-Navigator was created months ago. However, it has now existed for forty years..."

I took a deep breath at hearing this. Was it possible that *I* had actually engineered the Time Machine?

"Is this some sort of time-travelling riddle you're proposing? Or a bizarre joke?" asked the New York Times reporter. "How can such a machine have existed for forty years if you only finished making it last month?"

"It's not a joke or a riddle. It's an actual fact," said my future-self. "There is no difference between Time and any of the three dimensions of Space, except that *Time* exists in our consciousness. However, time does alter space, which is why the world's clocks are set differently. For instance, this room that we're in now is occupying space in London, but several hours from now this same space will be in New York because the world is turning on its axis. Similarly, where there were once mountain ranges millions of years ago, there are now oceans. Time alters Space.

"Yesterday I conducted an elaborate experiment. I visited the year 2011 with the aid of my machine and opened a company called *Time Unlimited*. Then, I posted a mail-order catalogue with the Time Machine listed in it through my own door, to my past-self, to see if I could stop my wife's murder while I was still fit, agile and young because I'm too old and frail to try now."

The New York Times reporter shook his head angrily. "This is ridiculous! Preposterous! I've never heard such an outlandish tale in all my life. Do you really expect us to believe such utter nonsense professor?"

I watched the other reporters come to their feet, shaking their heads too, voicing the same sentiments. They were heading for the door. "Ludicrous! Utter garbage! Drivel! And from a man of such high standing in the scientific community," they disparaged as I stood there musing over what had been said.

I stared across at my future-self, shaking his head in despair. "Ladies and gentlemen, please sit back down. I haven't finished my talk and you haven't seen what you came here to see," he said with a sigh.

The reporters stopped in their tracks and then went back to their seats looking puzzled while my future-self wore a satisfied smile, for it had occurred to him that there was more than one way to deal with his troublesome situation. "For the benefit of anyone who doubts my sincerity in what I've said tonight, I'm willing to give a demonstration, thus proving that the *Space-Time Continuum* really exists and can be traversed," he announced unequivocally. His tone was light, almost teasing.

One of the female reporters stared at him openly, admiringly, trying to frame her next question carefully. She was in her mid-forties, slender and dark, dressed stylishly. She raised her hand and smiled. "Professor, if a Time Machine really exists and you sent it back into the past to your younger-self, how are you going to prove any of this?"

I watched my future-self unclip a radio from his belt. He put it to his lips, pressed a button and it crackled into life. "Nav-Man, follow the *Timeline* I set earlier," he said.

Suddenly, there was a breath of wind in the room, even though no windows were open. The wall lights dimmed and went out leaving the room in complete darkness. Something began to glow in the gloom. Something shiny. Made of metal. Of colossal proportions. And it hummed and buzzed loudly. One of the female reporters screamed and fainted, falling to the floor with a dull thud. Whatever had appeared in the room shone like a bright red neon sign?

The temperature in the room rocketed to over 120 degrees making everyone sweat, except for me. I stared into the glaring red light and could just make out what looked like a robot, which was twice the size of a man in length, breadth and width. It was sinister, threatening and quite awesome to look at actually – in a primitive sort of way.

"Oh my God!" whimpered a female voice in the darkness. There was a loud scream. Then the lights came back on with a swiftness that stunned the reporters and everyone was staring at the colossal metal shape standing inanimate in the middle of the room, buzzing and crackling, surrounded by static electricity.

I watched my future-self blinking behind his horn-rimmed glasses, staring into the reporters' stunned, panic-stricken faces. "The structure of *Space-Time* is irregular, but quite predictable at a sub-atomic level and is known as the quantum state. It's what allows the passage of time through space in any direction – past, present or future. Matter is also transferred at the sub-atomic level in the same way, using the same principles, which is how my shiny metal friend arrived here a moment ago."

The reporters' jaws were hanging open, their eyes wide. All were speechless and unable to remove their unblinking gaze from the robot. Suddenly an alarm bell sounded startling everyone, including me. The reporters shot to their feet, looking even more panic stricken. "Don't concern yourselves, it's only my fire alarm going off because of the extreme temperature created by the robot's super-conductive metal core," announced my future-self. He walked over to the wall and pressed a small red button. The alarm stopped almost immediately, but it was still ringing in my ears.

The reporters sat back down and a blonde female raised her hand into the air. "Professor Ward, you're a well-known physicist who has studied at Cal-Tec and ITC Research in Black Rock, and it's been reported that you've been working with unknown metals with unique properties, which came to earth in the form of a meteorite. Is this robot a product of those newly discovered metals?"

"Super-Conducting Metals, my dear. And yes it is," agreed my future-self.

"Then what is the purpose of the robot?" asked the New York Times reporter.

My future-self stroked his goatee beard thoughtfully for a moment. "It's a *Time-Travelling, Crash-Dummy*, but a whole lot smarter!"

"Could you elaborate professor?" asked another reporter.

My future-self nodded and smiled. "Crash-Dummies are used by car manufacturers to establish the safety of a particular vehicle before it goes on the road. Nav-Man is the Time-Travelling equivalent of a Crash-Dummy. I built him specifically to establish whether time-travel is or isn't safe before trying it myself. I didn't dare go rushing off through the Fourth Dimension to the distant-past or far-flung future without knowing whether I might come to a sudden jarring halt inside something solid, smashing every molecule of my body to pieces. Therefore, I built the ultimate Crash-Dummy to take that dangerous journey into the unknown first."

The New York Times reporter shook his head in dismay. "Oh, this is *preposterous!* It's all..."

"Why?" interrupted my future-self.

"Because it's against all reason," said the reporter.

"What reason?" said my future-self.

"Anyone can argue that black is white, but you won't convince me that you have discovered *Time-Travel*," said the reporter. "Not even with all your wild extravagant theories!"

"I have never mentioned or talked about my experiments

until today, but I have called this press conference for experimental verification by yourselves," said my future-self.

"Then let's get on and be done with it, because my backside has no feeling anymore!" said the Daily Herald reporter. "Let's see your experiment and judge for ourselves whether it's all humbug or not!"

I watched my future-self smile round at the reporters with his hands deep in his trouser pockets, before turning his back on them. He walked slowly over to the robot. "What you are about to witness is no sleight-of-hand-trick or illusion. Nav-Man is as real as you or I and I need two volunteers to assist me. Come ladies and gentlemen of the world's press, who would like to be part of history in the making?"

Most of the reporters shook their heads. However, two did volunteer. A man and a woman. Both marched purposefully but pensively towards the robot, fear flashing in their eyes, and they halted in its shadow as it loomed over them menacingly.

"It is rather scary, isn't it?" said my future-self, laughing cheerily.

Both reporters stared at each other and then at my other-self. "Yes, *it* is!" they agreed in unison.

I watched my other-self pause briefly. Then he lifted the hand of the female reporter and made her point her forefinger towards a tiny lever on his portable radio. Meanwhile, he asked the male reporter to touch the robot on its sculpted breastplate, which he did nervously – and even though it looked red hot, it was ice cold.

"Surprised?" asked my other-self.

"Extremely so," said the male reporter.

"It took me two years to build and every ounce of brainpower," my other-self reported. "However, *Nav-Man,* as I've called him is my greatest achievement to date."

"Get on with this so-called experiment will you. I don't want to sit here and die of old age, listening to the two of you prattle on. It's all humbug anyway!" cried the New York Times reporter rudely.

I watched my future-self staring hard at the impatient reporter. However, there was a twinkle in his eye. "I want you all to understand that when your female colleague presses this little lever, Nav-Man will vanish and glide into the past. He will visit the year 2011 A.D., and return some moments later with proof of where he's been."

"What kind of proof?" asked the New York Times reporter.

"What proof would you like?" asked my other-self, matter-of-factly.

"Something rare that no one could possibly steal. Something from a museum or bank vault," said the reporter.

"The *Hope Diamond* perhaps? Or the *Mona Lisa?* Unless you have something even more specific in mind?" said my other-self. "You have endless possibilities to choose from!"

"The Hope Diamond will do just fine!" said the reporter with a gleam in his eyes.

Everyone was silent for a moment, their expressions thoughtful as we all watched my future-self nod to the female reporter. "Press the lever forward when you're ready my dear," he said. "All of you watch the robot and satisfy yourselves that there's no trickery involved in what I do, because I don't want to be called a quack or faker ever again."

We all watched the female press the lever. There was the familiar breath of wind in the room and the lights dimmed but didn't go out. Suddenly the robot swung around in a jerky movement and its black visor lifted, red eyes gleaming. It became indistinct, ghostlike for a second or two and there was an eddy of faint noises like the whirring of cogs and gears. Then it was gone! Vanished! Except for a pair of rather large footprints in the thick pile rug it had stood upon.

Again everyone was silent for a moment. Stunned.

The New York Times reporter shook his head in disbelief. "Well I'll be damned!" he whispered. The other reporters shot to their feet and walked over to the rug. They stared down at the large footprints and wafted their hands through the empty space where the robot had been moments earlier. At this, my future-self laughed cheerfully. "Well, what do you all think of that?" he said. He went to his drinks cabinet and poured himself a scotch with a splash of soda.

The reporters stared at each other. "Look here old chap, are you earnest about this? Do you seriously believe that monstrosity of a machine has travelled through *Time?* More to the point, do you expect us to believe it?"

My future-self nodded. "Certainly I do, on both counts," he replied. Stooping to light his fire with a match, he then produced a cigar and lit that too. Placing one hand in his deep trouser pocket, he turned back around to face the reporters with a satisfied grin on his face. Puzzled and incredulous they returned to their allotted seats and sat back down, staring at the vacant expression on my future-self's face as he puffed away on his fat cigar, blowing smoke rings into the air cockily.

"Look here old chap, do you seriously expect us to believe that this is *not* a trick of some sort?" said The Chicago Gazette reporter.

"I'm a physicist, not an illusionist," came the retort, "and I have never been more serious in my life!"

"Remarkable!" mumbled one of the female reporters.

My future-self spun his head to her. "Pardon my dear, did you say something?"

"I was just thinking out loud," she admitted. "I think the whole concept of what you have achieved is remarkable! Unbelievable even! Yet I do believe!"

My future-self winked at her and smiled. "Clever girl! Only eleven more to convert and convince then!"

"I like your lucid frankness about this whole affair professor. However, I suspect some subtle reserve in what you have demonstrated today. Is there something that you haven't told us?" asked the reporter with the wide mustache.

My other-self smiled faintly. "If I were Hollywood's favourite thriller writer, I could possibly evoke the amazing experience of time-travel superbly for you all. However, as I have said, I am a *physicist* and can only imagine the great risks a mortal person would take while making a journey through Time. Such an impossible journey. Made possible by my craftsmanship with metals from a different world." He looked at his watch. Five minutes had elapsed. "Where has that robot got to? It should have been back by now."

The New York Times reporter had seen and heard enough. "Balderdash! I've never sat through such twaddle. It's an abominable insult to my intelligence that you think I would fall for such an incredible piece of story-telling, even with that fake robot to hand!"

My future-self looked shocked at hearing this. "You doubt my sincerity?"

The Times reporter shook his head. "No! I doubt your sanity! And mine for listening to your *brilliantly imagined* story!"

I watched and waited, listening patiently to all sides of the rollicking argument, and most of the reporters left unconvinced, questioning my future-self's credentials and sanity. To make matters worse, the robot never came back. Was it lost in Time I wondered? Even my future-self didn't seem to know. I found out much later that its memory chip had burned out and a guidance module failed, leaving it to wander the centuries completely out of control, to create havoc wherever it appeared.

It did, however, have a homing-beacon integrated into its mechanism, but would it ever actually activate, bringing it home? I returned to the present day in Scotland, knowing that *I* had made the greatest discovery in the history of man, the Time Machine, and made the most complicated and awesome piece of machinery ever devised. Nav-Man!

Chapter 15

Not far away in the not so distant past, on a cold night, Terry and Frankie were passing by shoppers gathered to listen to the Salvation Army singers outside Top Shop, on High Street in Peckham, London, when suddenly Frankie halted and stared at one pretty female singer. *She's in a class of her own,* he thought. *Terrific face. Sensational figure. I must have her. Tonight!* He turned to face someone in the crowd of listeners. "What time do the singers finish?"

The young man stared oddly at Frankie and then looked at his wristwatch. The fluorescent dial glowed in the dark. "It's 9:15 p.m., so they'll be here for another hour," he said, turning his head back to listen to the singers.

Frankie smiled. *I'll be back in an hour then,* he thought. He stared at the young woman again and she smiled his way. His pulse was now in the red zone, and would remain so until he satisfied his craving for the thrill of the kill. However, he fully intended to pleasure himself first while torturing her. There would be terrific shocks. Horrific sensations. Screams galore. And an intense atmosphere that would make him feel in a class of his own. His pulse raced harder at the thought. He closed his eyes and tried to breathe, imagining what was to come later. He opened them again. "Come on, let's go for a beer across the road," he said, tugging at Terry's arm and he began crossing the road with his friend following. It had been a long, eventful, tiring day and Terry was ready for a beer.

Inside the bar, Frankie was preoccupied by trying to shoo away a fly that persistently buzzed around his head, and by the time it moved off, Terry had been served and was heading for a circular table with two vacant chairs. They both sat down and sighed, staring at each other.

"You wanna hear a funny joke?" Frankie suddenly blurted.

Terry sipped at his beer and nodded. "Yeah, I could do with a laugh."

Frankie put his hands together on the table and cracked his knuckles. "What's the difference between a *wank* and a *tank*?" he asked dryly.

Terry smiled. "No idea, what?"

Frankie grinned, put a finger in his mouth and made a pop. "You can hear a tank comin'!" He chuckled.

Terry broke out into a voluptuous drowning laughter that filled the barroom and customers stared momentarily, but then went back about their business.

"That's pretty funny," Terry admitted. "Tell me another."

Frankie grinned. "What do you have if you're holding a *green ball* in each hand?"

Terry shook his head, looking puzzled. "I have no idea!"

Frankie's grin widened. "The Incredible Hulk, right where you want him!"

Terry chuckled cheerily and they spent the next forty-five minutes cracking jokes and poking fun at the customers – something that Frankie did wherever he went, in the hope of provoking a fight if he could. Finally, Frankie made his excuses and left the bar on the pretext of being tired and drunk. He was neither. He was, however, hot and excited at the prospect of what was to come in the next few hours.

It was cold outside and the Salvation Army singers were packing up their instruments, but unfortunately for Frankie, the young woman was nowhere to be seen. He inhaled sharply, looking panicked. Now he zipped up and down the pavement searching for her. Suddenly, there was a piercing shriek and his eyes darted across the road. It was her. She had slipped on the ice and hit the pavement hard. Frankie ran across the road, unable to believe his good fortune. Now he stood over her in freeze-frame with his hand held out towards her. "Let me give you a hand up?" he offered finally.

She was lying on her back. Rolling over onto her side she took several deep breaths and the pain she felt showed on her face. "Ouch!" she said, looking dazed. Reaching out he leaned over her and she took his hand. He hauled her to her unsteady feet and could smell her sweet fragrant perfume. It seemed intoxicating. His pulse raced like it had an hour ago when he had first spotted her through the crowd of onlookers.

Staring into her beautiful sparkling eyes, several torn bodies floated before him, hauntingly. Closing his eyes he counted to three. He opened them again. "My God, your knees are bleedin'. That must have been a heck of a fall you took lady."

She glanced down at her knees. They were red, bruised and swollen, her tights torn and a mess. With trembling fingers she touched the cuts and winced. "Oh, my Lord, not good," she whispered.

Frankie squatted to pick up her handbag and he gave it back to her with his best do-gooder smile. *She's not suspicious of my intentions,* he thought, smiling weakly. *She's hurt and half-frozen.* He smiled again. "My name's Frankie and I live quite close if you wanna clean yourself up?"

She stared at him for a moment. "I wouldn't mind, if it's no trouble."

"No trouble at all, I'll even throw in a bite to eat."

"That's very kind of you, my name's Molly."

Nice one! She's fallen for it. Hook, line and sinker, he thought. *Now I am gonna get a fuck!* "Come on then, it's just around the corner." *And that's all there is to kidnapping someone, you stupid bitch.*

Frankie strode out and she trotted at his heels, limping. It was raining heavily now and both were shivering by the time they reached his digs. Once inside, he went to his bedroom and took off his wet clothes, throwing on a wooly sweater and a pair of old jogging bottoms. Then he went back to the living room where Molly was sitting on a less than comfy couch, holding her grazed knees. He went off into the kitchen to make her a cold turkey sandwich, and while she was scoffing it, he slipped up behind her and hit her over the head with a heavy frying pan. Her lights went out.

***

IN THE BASEMENT there was shouting and screaming. "You whore bitch, I *am* gonna fuck you!" rang out loud and clear. There were more screams. No one could hear them. Frankie had done a good job of sound-proofing the place. Molly, her hands tied firmly behind her back, was standing facing Frankie using all kinds of colourful language, and then she spat in his face. He grabbed her, tearing her dress and threw her to the cold stone floor. He was drunk now. And when he was drunk he was even more vicious and violent – as violent as any man could be. He threw himself on top of her, tearing off what was left of her dress and she screamed again.

"Get off me, you animal!" she snapped as he ripped into her with his manhood. But the more she struggled and swore at him, the more he forced himself into her.

He shook his head. "No! I'm fuckin' you! You're mine now and I own your ass!" he snapped back, his voice slurred.

She shook her head too. "Let me go, you bastard!" she screamed.

Then for a single moment he lay on top of her unmoving, and the smell of his sweaty flesh against hers and the horror of what he was forcing her to do made her sick. She brought up the turkey sandwich. He rolled away from the vomit onto his side, eyes wide. Then he grabbed her, hauling him and her back to their feet, hitting her mouth with his clenched fist. He growled at her like a wild animal, throwing her down onto an airbed like a rag doll and he raped her for what seemed like

like an eternity.

Finally, when he'd finished, she opened her eyes filled with tears. She screamed. Laughing drunkenly he ripped into her again while holding onto her arms, pumping his body up and down on top of her shouting, "Take that! And that! And that, you whore bitch!" Finally satisfied, he rolled away from her onto his side.

Molly was crying fitfully now, whispering, "May God forgive you, because I won't, you bastard. I hope you die!" She vomited again.

He laughed wickedly, hauled himself upright and then bent and grabbed her by the wrists, dragging her to her feet. "No more!" she screamed hysterically. However, he swung his arm in a stiff arc and hit her in the face with his clenched fist, knocking her to the floor. He did it again. And again, shouting that she *was* a whore-bitch that must be beaten. Then he slit her throat and buried her in a corner, after pouring lime over her body.

***

IN THE PRESENT DAY, somewhere secret in Norfolk, Sir Jeremy Collins-Smyth, his manner sullen, spoke in a low nasal voice. Still dressed in his favourite Harris Tweed suit and tweed hat, he paced the length of the top security facility aided by a walking stick. Finally he spoke. "If I wanted to creep around finding out what other people are up to, or sneak into places I shouldn't go, or send secret messages to other agents, pass unseen through crowded streets, listen to conversations that I shouldn't have access to, and poke my nose into everything that's none of my damn business – how would I manage to do it all without being discovered?" he asked.

A young, green, snot-nosed agent raised his hand. "Sir, spying is one of the world's oldest professions and one of the most dangerous, but a good spy can change the world – and several already have. Example: it wasn't a scientist who figured out the secrets of the H-bomb for the Russians. It was a spy who stole them from the Americans. And it wasn't political arguments or dire threats that brought American troops in, to help the Allies during World War One; it was a coded message, cracked by a British spy. So, the answer to your question is – be a *great* spy!"

Sir Jeremy nodded to the young agents in his class. "Give that man a cigar! Fantastic answer!" he congratulated. "It will now be incorporated in the confidential – top secret – Spy's Handbook." He laughed cheerily. "And to prove the young man's assumption that spying is one of the oldest professions – if not the oldest – I can tell you that even Moses dispatched field agents to spy out the land of Canaan, to bring back information on the people who lived there, on whether it was worth taking from them. Check out Chapter thirteen of the Book of Numbers in the Old Testament and you will see for yourselves.

"Also, it is as he stated; one of the most dangerous professions. Spies are assassinated regularly in various ways – by poison, electrocution, hanging, decapitation or gassing. The lucky few are jailed for life. So, before you guys turn up the collars of your raincoats, pull down the brims of your Homburgs, or put on your dark glasses, I want you to know that it is an interesting profession, but a deadly one!"

The classroom was packed to the rafters and all were listening intently to Sir Jeremy's dulcet, even if somewhat nasal tones. However, unseen to the naked eye, there was an uninvited guest made completely of an unknown, otherworldly alloy, listening intently to the making and breaking of codes and secret messages, and the whys and wherefores of bugging and tailing other agents, and a whole lot more.

Sir Jeremy lectured the agents on astounding cases. How to set up a spy ring. Disguising messages. Body language and the art of eavesdropping, plus many other useful things, including beating a lie detector test. Questions were asked and answers given, and all the while their uninvited guest watched and listened too. There was an irony here. Sir Jeremy, the ultimate spy was being spied upon and he didn't suspect a thing. But then, how could he? The robot was in its spectral form.

Finally, with the lecture over, the robot materialised, raised its visor and laid waste to the whole classroom, killing every single agent with its lasers, chopping them to pieces, including Sir Jeremy. Only a blood-spattered, blackened, smouldering room remained.

***

IN THE PRESENT DAY I'd had my fill of the Scottish Highlands and headed back to my flat in London to plan my final assault on Time. I now believed that I could kidnap Jane's murderer from the past and get rid of him once and for all, by dumping his ass in the far-flung future. And I was almost certain that Frankie *was* the murderer. His psychotic profile fitted the bill perfectly, and he had been in Fat Jack's bar on the night of the murder.

I had now discovered that *Time Travel* was like parachuting, which I had done in my younger days – get the first jump over with and it becomes almost routine. However, you must never become complacent and must always check your parachute every time. And so, before I travelled anywhere, I checked my facts down to the finest detail. This became a habit. A good one. Because it would be too easy to end up encased in rock or at the bottom of the sea if my calculations were wrong.

I stared out of the living room window. Rain lashed the

London landscape and the wind howled as I switched my gaze to Jane's portrait hanging on the far wall. She *was* so beautiful, and would have been so even in old age. We would have finally settled down to a quiet life, in a quiet village somewhere, and doted on our grandchildren, but I'd had all that snatched away from me by a murdering maniac and had buried the only woman I ever truly loved. *I've always loved you and still do.*

Switching my gaze back to the window, the London lights winked at me through the rain. Staring at them for a long time I stood up and walked over to the portrait, plucking it from the wall, tracing the contours of Jane's face with my forefinger until it finally rested upon her lips. I kissed them and began to cry because I knew she was so happy with her life the last time I saw her alive. So happy being with me. I cried for hours and finally fell asleep, where once again I watched her die over and over again in my horrific nightmares.

But then I awoke with a start and it was morning. I stood up from the couch stiffly and shuffled along the parquet floor, down the hallway and went into the bathroom where I used the toilet, then the shower to freshen up. I went to the bedroom next, dressed quickly, putting on a blue shirt and black trousers with a needle-sharp crease and polished shoes. Glancing at my wristwatch I noted the time. It was 11:00 p.m. Now my gaze switched to the mirror on the dresser and somehow I looked frightened, but then, I was about to become *Judge, Jury* and *Executioner*.

Chapter 16

I put on my Homburg and black overcoat. I was ready to go back to the night Jane went missing and I wasn't returning to the present day without changing what had happened to her. I wanted her back. I went to the bedroom and picked up the Time Machine from my dresser drawer, unlocking the leather case. Switching it on the familiar voice asked, "Space Time Coordinates?"

I set the machine for July 26th 2008. However, this time I set it for slightly earlier that evening and gave verbal commands that were very specific. Pressing the buttons I waited. Suddenly, there seemed a breath of wind and the lights flickered once or twice as the room became indistinct and my reflection in the mirror became hazy. *Ghostlike.* Flickering in and out of sight. Then everything was silent for a moment as my reflection vanished completely from the mirror. There was a loud click, a dull drone, and my mind reeled from the mad feeling of falling weightlessly through time. I had entered the Fourth Dimension and my mind went numb as the room spun wildly. Everything seemed to be a ghostly blur and I was sick to my stomach. But as wandered further and further back in time, I once again saw visions of trains, planes and all the modern things that had been invented, and then watched them smash into a million pieces in one great collision and passed out. I was glad, because it stopped that awful, sickly, falling feeling.

Suddenly, there was a flash of blinding light and a great confusion of noise around me. My eyes popped open. I was back outside Fat Jack's bar on the night my wife went missing and I was in a solid form. I walked around the red exterior and leaned against the rough brick. The wind was cold, the sky clear and stars were sparkling brightly like tiny diamonds.

Suddenly, there were footsteps on the walkway behind me and I turned, hunched, glancing back, watching Terry and Frankie approaching as I had done on a previous occasion. My blood chilled. Frankie was laughing, but they passed by without noticing me in the shadows again. Frankie's face shone eerily in the glare of the red neon-lights of the bar's side window and he looked crazier than ever. They turned the corner and entered the bar, still laughing and joking.

As before, I had double-checked my facts in the police reports. This *was* the last place my wife was seen alive, and Frankie and Terry were the last customers to leave the bar, literally moments after my wife and her best friend Vicky had. That spoke volumes. Images and sounds exploded before my eyes and in my mind as had happened the time before – I saw and heard the shooting of the barman in Fat Jack's; the terrified face of the woman in the farmhouse they were going to rob and kill; the maniacal laughter echoing throughout the museum they had broken into. All of it seemed like a ghastly nightmare. Nevertheless, it *was* starkly real! I came back to myself, still leaning on the wall.

Then, as before, the *EXIT* door to the bar slammed open, hitting me like a jack-hammer in the back. I slid down the wall and ended up sprawled on the concrete as the same huge coloured guy brought out the trash and dumped it in the alleyway right in front of me. "You okay?" he asked, looking down at me, slightly perturbed.

This time I refrained from saying, "No, I'm bloody well not, you clumsy oaf!" Instead I just staggered back to my feet, brushing myself down.

He smiled weakly. "You really shouldn't be standin' there, you could get badly hurt!" Slamming the heavy metal door shut behind him, he went back inside.

I walked back around the corner slowly, staring at the

fluorescent dial on my watch shining in the dark. It was close to midnight. Suddenly, a black cab pulled over to the curb and screeched to a halt. The door flung open immediately and my wife and Vicky jumped out. I ducked back into the shadows of the alleyway before they could see me and my eyes misted and tears rolled down my cheeks. The lump in my throat made it hard to swallow as old memories of great times we'd shared flared in my mind. Consciously, I forced myself to push them to one side. My feelings were still raw and hurt like hell, but there she was, even more beautiful than I remembered. My pulse was in the red zone. I placed the Time Machine in my deep coat pocket, but left it switched on just in case I needed to make a quick getaway.

It began to rain heavily and each drop was stained red by the neon lights, reminding me of Jane's bloodied and battered body. I gave a sigh and a cough, throaty and moist and my eyes misted again. I sniffed back the tears just in time to see my wife and Vicky go into Fat Jack's. Cold air stung my throat as I almost called out for her not to go into the bar. However, I restrained myself and didn't. I wouldn't have been able to explain my presence here, or why I was watching and following her, and I was now confident that I could change what was going to happen to her with the help of my tiny, shiny machine.

I marched around to the front of the bar and peered through the window. Shocked I was. My wife and Vicky were sitting opposite Terry and Frankie and they were all laughing. To an outsider it might have looked like an innocent, cosy scene. However, I was horrified. My mind went into overdrive. *Did Jane and Vicky know Terry and Frankie? Had they met before?* I began gasping for breath, aghast, screaming inside. *Was she having an affair at the time of her murder,* I wondered? It was really cold out now, but I was actually sweating, feeling physically sick at the thought. *Could I have been so wrong about my marriage? My life? My wife?*

I pushed the hurtful thoughts from my mind. *Don't be silly. I'm a lawyer for Christ's sake, think like one! It's as innocent as it looks. Frankie and Terry are just trying it on with the girls. They won't respond, I'm sure of it!* I pushed my face closer to the stained glass window, almost flattening my nose, my eyes wide. Then my heart missed a beat when Frankie took Jane's left hand and kissed the back of it. A cold chill descended upon me and seemed to settle in my bones. Now something hot and heavy stirred in my chest and my heart sank as he took her other hand, pulling her closer. Then to my utter horror, he kissed her full on the lips. I closed my eyes. *No!* I screamed inside. *This isn't happening! It can't be!*

I staggered back from the window in shock and trudged down the road, peering into dark doorways and entrances shouting, *"No!"* over and over again, feeling physically sick. After a while I came to a deep doorway and slumped into it, wondering if I'd really seen what I'd seen. It was late. I was tired. I could have been hallucinating, but then I heard footsteps in the dark. Footsteps and laughter. My eyes were closed tightly, but I opened them. Then the words, "We can go to my place," rang in the air.

"You fascinate me," a female voice replied.

To my utter horror, I recognised it as Jane's voice. My living nightmare was getting worse by the second. I placed my hand into my coat pocket and took out the Time Machine as the footsteps came closer. Opening my eyes I peered around the doorway, just in time to see Frankie staring into my wife's eyes, while making suggestive comments about how he could make her feel like a million dollars. She laughed rather innocently, I thought. But then, *she* kissed him full on the lips. Closing my eyes again, I staggered back into the recesses of the doorway, inwardly screaming *"No!"* I hit the button on the machine to return me to the present day. And just before I made the leap back to my own time – with a broken heart – I noticed the same staring red eyes I'd seen before. They were watching me from an ally across the street. Then I blacked out.

I awoke with a start, drenched in sweat, my heart beating like a hammer in my chest. I was laid out on the living room floor, squinting my eyes, focusing them on the clock above the fire, noting the time. It was 11:01 am. I'd been gone for no more than a minute, but my whole life had come crashing down around me in just sixty seconds. Now, I had no wife and a world-full of even more hurtful memories.

I had seen a lot of movies where the hero's life had fallen apart, taken one bad turn after another, and that's just how my life felt right now. But in the movies, the hero usually wins the day, gets the girl, ends up smelling of roses and loaded with cash! Whereas I had lost my wife, my life, probably my kids and given up a great career – and all in under a fortnight! With this record, if I offered my lawyer services to a sleazy, greasy cafe, they would turn me down, I'm sure. Maybe the Time Machine is a *curse* and not a Godsend. After all, I wouldn't have seen Frankie kissing my wife and be in purgatory right now if I hadn't got it.

***

NOT FAR AWAY in another time and another place.

"...How much time have you done in the slammer, Frankie," the doctor asked.

"Loads! More than I care to remember!"

"What for?"

"Fighting. Drunk and disorderly. Burglary. Grand theft. Rape. Attempted *murder.*"

"That's quite a list and quite an admission. You are by all accounts, habitually a criminal and a dangerous threat to society without your medication. You *must* keep taking the prescribed medication to stop your desires."

Frankie didn't admit that he had stopped taking the medication months ago, or the fact that he had killed a number of times in recent months. Nor did he admit that he would have loved to have been a soldier, whose chief function *is* to kill the enemy, do in lives, or whatever you want to call it. To Frankie, this is where the distinctions get blurred. The killing of the enemy by a soldier is not murder. You don't go to jail for it. In fact, the government sometimes gives you a medal, which is why it would have suited him right down to the ground.

I'm not a murderer, he thought, sitting there in the red leather, reclining chair. *I'm a soldier out of uniform, performing a duty, killing for my country – disposing of evil women as and when I can.*

The doctor stopped writing his notes, lifted his head and stared hard at Frankie. "Have you ever committed a murder and gotten away with it?" he asked as if uncannily reading the other's mind.

Frankie stared back at him twice as hard. "If the law can't prove it, then I ain't done it!" He laughed; eyes wide, a mad stare on his face.

***

IN THE PRESENT DAY, in London, I had decided to go back in time to stop Frankie being born. I'd had enough pain, heartache and misery and just wanted an end to it all, after seeing what I'd seen. I couldn't stand the thought of her being with Frankie. That was sick. It hurt even more than knowing she was dead. However, when I went back in time and stopped him from being born, by introducing his mother to a different man, instead of his father, it caused a *time paradox.* When I came back to the present day, Jane was happily married to another man and they were leading an idyllic lifestyle together. I was devastated. At my wit's end.

Then, something even worse happened. Time rippled, warped and split, and I was lost in the split, my machine gone forever, or so I thought, leaving me stranded in a kind of ethereal limbo. I *was* lost in time and space. But then the Time Machine returned to me after what seemed an eternity, because fortunately I had removed the homing-beacon and had it in my pocket. Finally, I used the key on the side of the machine to undo what I had done to cause the destructive time-paradox and everything returned to normal, thank God.

Now I realised that the past is always present and *can* be changed, but it's very dangerous to do so. However, against my better judgment I decided there and then, that no matter how dangerous it was, it would not stop me from propelling myself into the Fourth Dimension in the hope of changing my past, thus getting my beautiful wife back. I just had to fine tune the past and possibly the present, in order to alter my future for the better.

I thought back to the last time I made love to Jane, two nights before her disappearance. It had started off as a pillow fight and escalated playfully into something much more serious and passionate. I remember gazing at her more than ample breasts and began experiencing a pull from the pit of my stomach, which turned into a tingling alertness at the sight of her swelling nipples through her silk pajamas, and I could tell she was getting the same horny feelings.

We were so alike. Kindred spirits in everything, particularly love making. It was always an equal mix of heavenly passion and raw animal sex. We'd kiss indulgently, flowingly and it was a feeling like no other. My heart would thunder out of control as our lips fused together, and then my hands would span her waist, pulling her closer and she would nuzzle into me, kissing *my* nipples, arousing me even more. I'd do the same to her. There was no: 'does that feel good to you'? We knew it did! And her arms would tighten around my shoulders as if she never wanted to let me go. Then our naked flesh would fuse too, for what seemed an eternity as I stroked and kissed her satin smooth skin, while we made passionate love over and over again.

Suddenly, I came back from my thoughts and began to cry, the sad feelings being indescribable. How do you mend a broken heart? You can't is the simple answer! I walked over to my wall bar and poured a rather large scotch with a splash of water and then I picked up our wedding album, opening it as I sat down on the sofa.

The first photograph was of Jane arriving at St Stevens' church in a 1954 Bentley, R-Type Continental, one of only 208 ever made and she looked amazing in her white veiled dress. I had never seen a bride looking so beautiful, *ever*. My breath caught in my throat that day as she climbed out of the Bentley with her father holding her hand, exclaiming, "*Wow! What a car!*"

I remember thinking: *it's got six cylinders and has a 4.5-litre engine. It's fitted with central locking, climate control, satellite navigation and a host of other self-indulgent conveniences, but you can keep the car, because Jane looks like a million dollars, is too hot for climate-control, acts like a mistress rather than a wife, looks like an angel in a bridle-gown, but sizzles like the devil in bed! Wow!*

I began to cry again at my loss. I wanted to kill myself, but then my subconscious told me to be calm and controlled. I didn't want to be calm or controlled, so I tossed the wedding album across the room with all my strength, smashing a mirror to pieces on the far wall, besides knocking over a standard lamp as the album fell to the floor with a dull thud.

Photographs were scattered everywhere and the room was littered with shards of glass from the mirror. I hate it when I let my temper get the better of me, but sometimes I think I'll explode if I don't let the anger out, one way or another. I stood up and walked to the wall bar, pouring myself another scotch, leaving the mess where it lay. I tossed my head back, polishing off the scotch in one large gulp and poured another, and then another, until I felt completely sozzled – drunk out of my frickin' mind. It was at this time that I decided to win the lottery to cheer myself up.

Chapter 17

Well, winning seven million pounds is bound to make an unbearable life a little more bearable, don't you think? It was easy. In the present day I simply jumped forward in time to Saturday, saw the winning numbers being picked and jumped back to Friday to buy my lottery ticket with the winning numbers on it. It was harmless fun and a great distraction from the pain of my loss.

Both of my grandfathers were self-made men – one a country lad who retired a millionaire at the age of forty, from the business he had created, and the other an office boy who climbed the ladder of success to become the owner of a steel smelting company worth millions. It took years. I fiddled with *Time* and became a millionaire in less than twenty-four hours. But I was still miserable.

And so, I hid myself away for the next two years, trying to forget what I'd seen and heard that day in the alley behind Fat Jack's bar, and I began taking my medication again and resumed therapy with Dr. Aldrich. I even stopped Time Travelling. Instead, I wrote novels, mostly about my present day experiences as a lawyer, but I never managed to get any of them published. Maybe I should have written them about my experiences in Time. People would think them fiction, but I would know they were fact, and I bet they would be published and sell millions.

However, most people consider Time Travel impossible, but wouldn't you have considered air travel impossible if you had been living a hundred and fifty years ago? I know I would, and I have a completely open mind. But, it's strange how the human mind has limits.

***

IN THE PAST, Terry and Frankie were arguing.

"Take... take your Goddam hands off me," Frankie gasped. His dark eyes blazed, his face was deathly white and only a superhuman effort enabled him to keep his clenched fists pressed to his sides. In another second he would have hit Terry.

The barkeeper forced them apart. "What's this all about?" he snapped.

Angrily, Terry strode to the other side of the bar where he sat down on a stool, rolling a cigarette. Lighting it with a strip-match he inhaled deeply, glancing back over at Frankie. Then he struck the bar top with his clenched fist. "Get your ass over here so I can talk to you!" he snapped.

Frankie shook his head. "Nothin' to talk about!"

"Get over here, or I'll come and slap you silly, you son-of-a-bitch."

Frankie's shoulders slumped and he shook his head again. "No!"

"I'm not askin' you. I'm tellin' you to get here now, we need to talk!" Terry's face was a picture of anger, his eyes ablaze.

Frankie turned in a temper, smoothing one hand over his dark hair and he marched across the bar to where Terry was, sitting down beside him on a bar-stool. He too rolled a cigarette and lit it, finally blowing smoke rings in the air.

Terry spun on his stool. "You're an ignorant fool. After months of planning this new caper, you nearly get nicked for shopliftin' ciggies, you twat!"

A quick, sickly smile spread over Frankie's face. "Oh, come on, stop exaggeratin', no one fuckin' spotted me!"

"You're missing the point as usual. They might have!"

Frankie's reaction was predictable. "Yeah, but no one did!"

"Have you ever thought about why you're such a loner? No, I bet you haven't! Well, I'll tell you why. It's because you're too hot to handle. Even in jail no one wanted to associate themselves with you, because you lose the plot and wanna kill for no apparent reason. Most people have a fuse. You don't. You just fuckin' explode, destroying and laying waste to everyone and everything in the immediate vicinity. In fact, I could do less damage with a dozen fuckin' hand-grenades!"

Frankie laughed, but looked annoyed.

Terry closed his eyes as he drew on his cigarette and exhaled loudly. "I'd pay good money to see you stay calm in a sticky situation."

It took every ounce of self-control Frankie had, not to lash out at Terry where he sat. Friend or no friend. "It's probably better that I go now," he announced, stubbing his cigarette out on the bar top. He didn't look up.

"Ok," said Terry. "But where are you going?"

Frankie climbed from his stool and headed for the door. "I've an appointment with pretty face. Be seein' ya!"

***

MEANWHILE IN THE PRESENT DAY I considered having myself committed to an asylum, because even with the therapy and medication, my suffering wouldn't stop. I considered suicide again too. I even wrote letters to my long suffering children, and as I did so I ran my fingertips over the paper where I had pressed so hard out of sheer frustration at not knowing what to write, that my pencil tip broke. Well, just how do you tell your loved ones that you want to kill yourself – no matter what the reason? I screwed the paper up and binned it.

In the end I decided that even if I did kill myself, I'd be damned, go to hell and be in even more purgatory. Great! I don't believe in God anymore, but the *Devil* exists and has made all the difference to my sanity. Only a few people would be lucky enough to realise this sobering, scary thought.

What you've just read probably doesn't make any sense to a rational person, but I'm not rational anymore. I'm not even sure I'm *SANE!* Now, when I look in the mirror my eyes are sharp and piercing, my chin appears square, my nose more hawk-like, and it's as if I'm seeing a different person for the very first time. And it's getting harder to express my feeling for Jane, because of what I witnessed behind Fat Jack's bar.

Now, whole conversations between Jane and I drifted around in my head, taking on bizarre and sinister shapes. I remember how she would sometimes look rather strangely at me over her glasses and say, "No one really knows their *significant other* that well." Was she talking about not knowing me, or me not understanding her? Had I missed vital signs in our relationship, making me believe we were divinely happy, when if the truth be told, I was, but she wasn't? Could I really have been that insensitive, that stupid and that blissfully ignorant? Could I? And looking back now, the answer is *yes*, I could have been, because I seem to have lost the plot.

Also, looking back now, I had first believed that the Time Machine had given my life fresh purpose with a dazzling sequence of events, which might culminate in saving my wife's life – but things are far more complicated than that. And so is the passage of Time. Decision making is also a funny thing. You don't have to talk yourself into the right ones; you just know they're right!

Suddenly, my father's voice drifted into my mind. *"Do things with the highest of honour and the greatest of responsibility and you won't go far wrong in life, my boy"*, he once told me when I was taking the Bar Exam to become a lawyer, and that's the way I've run my life ever since.

So with that thought in mind, I once again propelled myself into the past, back three years, now weak and childishly afraid that my plan to stop my wife's murder would once again fail.

However, to *try* was a compulsion like no other, and at least now I had my faithful friend – the Time Machine – with me through the many trials and tribulations.

Now, as before, there was a flash of blinding light, my eyes popped wide open and I found myself in a solid form in the shadowy recesses of a doorway behind Fat Jack's bar, waiting and watching like some predatory creature from the dark realms of a nightmare. And it was at this time I realised that God *does* exist, all powerful and unseen, and that all the harm in the world is caused by man's own *free will* and the bad choices we make in life when we ignore the Lord's commandments. This in itself was a huge revelation to me after denying the Creator for so long. Man, even though made in God's image is his own worst enemy, and some men have the devil in them and are just pure evil like Frankie.

I stood up slowly and walked around the red brick exterior and leaned against the wall with the wind cold against my face. The sky was clear and the stars shining brightly overhead as I hid in the shadows. Suddenly, there were footsteps on the walkway behind me and I turned, hunched, glancing back, watching Terry and Frankie approaching as I eerily relived the past once again.

Frankie, his face shining in the glare of the neon lights was laughing as they passed me by unnoticed.

"Gotta surprise!" I heard him tell Terry in a whispered voice.

"Great, I love surprises," Terry whispered back. "What is it?"

Frankie smiled. "Got a fuck-buddy called Vicky for your birthday, seeing as how I forgot to get anything last year."

Terry's face hardened and he stopped dead in his tracks. He turned to face Frankie, staring down at him. "You're jokin' right?"

Frankie shook his head stiffly. "No, why?" he said looking genuinely surprised.

"Because I brought you here to talk about our next caper, not to fool around with women!" snapped Terry.

At this point, I'd seen and heard enough. There was a loose brick at my feet, so I picked it up and lunged forward striking Terry on the back of his head, knocking him out cold. Frankie stared at me in disbelief with his mouth hanging open, and then he reached into his coat pocket, producing a gun. Without even thinking, I knocked it from his hand with the brick. He winced, clutching his hand; it was bleeding from the strike. I dropped the brick and grabbed him around the throat with one hand and pulled the Time Machine out of my pocket with the other, turning it on. The screen lit up immediately and the familiar voice asked, "Where to, Time Traveller?"

Without even thinking I said, "Take me and this murdering monster to the future, to the last day of Earth's life – do it now!"

The Time Machine buzzed and vibrated, its gears and mechanisms clicking away in overdrive, and just for a split second before it activated, I saw a black cab pull over to the curb. Jane and Vicky jumped out and then I was overcome by the familiar falling feeling of weightlessness and everything spun wildly.

Suddenly, there was a flash of light and we were there, thirty million years hence. Eddying flakes of snow were dancing before my eyes, blowing on a moaning wind, and the Earth was now no more than an ice ball. Our sun was in its final death throws as I'd witnessed once before, and we watched it swelling into a red giant, engulfing mercury, then Venus, the darkness around us growing apace. I watched one of the sun's giant solar flares strike out into the universe, covering a million miles in the blink of an eye, and I cannot convey the sense of abominable desolation that hung over the planet as the eastern sky reddened with the sun looming so close that you could almost touch it. Frankie's eyes were wide, shining with fear, not understanding what was happening to him.

"You're doomed, you son-of-a bitch!" I snapped, watching him quiver and shake like a jelly. There wasn't a smile on his face now. He wasn't laughing either. But I was! I had longed for this moment, this final encounter. And it couldn't cause a Time Paradox, because for the Earth – there was no more *Time*. "Enjoy your last few seconds of life!" I announced, darkly exultant, unable to feel any spark of humanity towards Frankie or any remorse for what I was doing.

Very inhuman, you might think. But it was no more inhuman than what he was planning to do to Jane, if I had let him. Well, I wasn't going to let him slake his thirst for murder this time, or ever again.

Frankie shivered as the darkness around us flickered and thickened, and I watched him stare in horror through wide disbelieving eyes at the awesome spectacle before him. Then I departed like a ghost, leaving him watching Earth's last day ever, and the sounds of his cries were pitiful and dismal. But he was getting exactly what he deserved, because he had robbed, raped and murdered, and the beauty of it was, that nothing on Earth could stop his demise from happening. And so, his last moments of life would make him a witness to the *Greatest Show on Earth* – the end of the Solar System.

I came back to the present, through a blinking succession of thirty million days and nights, watching the dials upon my machine spinning backwards frantically. Finally, I saw my ghostly indistinct figure reappear in front of the mirror above the mantelpiece, and I strode over to my window looking out, seeing all the things I loved. I went to the bar and poured myself a scotch and water and sat down on the couch. It all seemed like a fanciful dream. Yet it seemed so unreasonable to assume that something very strange hadn't occurred. I remember yawning and rubbing my eyes, and then a silky female voice from behind me asked, "Where on earth have you been? Have you seen the time? Your medication is overdue!"

I spun my head around in the direction of the voice. It was Jane! She was back, safe and sound! And that's how it all happened.

"That's truly an incredible story! Fascinating! Spellbinding even!" said Dr. Aldrich. Then he shook his head solemnly. "And what's even more fascinating is that you actually believe it all happened. The medication isn't helping matters I think. You're far more delusional than I first thought. *You* killed your wife in a fit of jealous rage because she was having affairs with several different men, and your time-travelling-self is just a wishful dream you've invented to deal with your murderous feelings and the reality of what you did to Jane on that awful night, three years ago. The prescription drugs seemed to have helped you invent the whole far-fetched scenario, making it as real as... well … as real as you needed it to be to distract you from your hurtful memories. You are, of course, insane!"

I stared at the doctor. *You're the one who's nuts! I have the machine in my pocket right now!*

"When are you going to admit that you committed the crime you're locked up for? When are you going to stop this self-denial and move forward? You are crazy. Mad as Hatter! You're *not* a Time Traveller! Stop listening to the voices in your head and listen to me, and then I can take the straightjacket off."

Dr. Aldrich turned to the warder looking after me and I

heard him whisper, "Poor crazy fool. All he ever does is try to reach his trouser pocket."

Well, if I can reach my damn pocket, I'll bloody well show you that I'm not crazy.

Dr. Aldrich turned his head, staring at me with a look of pity. Then the lights flickered twice and went out and two laser like eyes shone in the dark. Something cold, made of metal touched him. He screamed. The guard screamed. Then the lights came back on suddenly and both Dr. Aldrich and the guard vapourised right before my eyes, and a metallic sounding voice announced, "Come with me, Time Traveller, now... we have all the time in the world!"

Or am I *CRAZY* and I *IMAGINED* that too...?

To be Continued in: ***...TIME AND TIME AGAIN...***

Acknowledgment

A very special thank you to my brother, Frank, whose passion was all knowledge – God rest his soul. His photographic memory and instant recall helped me put so many pieces of this puzzle together, particularly his insights into the 1930's gangster era of the Central United States and the lawlessness of the Great Depression, besides so many other interesting facts, which I hope make this novella a... *great read...*

About the Author.

Michael Siddall was born in Sheffield, South Yorkshire, England, and his aspirations to become a novelist began after devising the board game, 'A Challenge of the Gods'.

Educated at Newfield School in Sheffield, he left with exemplary grades in his final exams and went on to Granville College for two years, where he studied literature, art, design and history. Times were hard and he left college to become a carpet fitter.

As a child of nine years Michael contracted Rheumatic Fever, spending a whole year in the Northern General Hospital laid flat on his back for the first six months and in a wheelchair for the following six. To occupy himself he wrote his first short stories and poems and has continued to write every day of his life since.

He was told that as a consequence of his illness he would have a weak heart and spend the rest of his life in a wheelchair. Michael proved the specialists wrong. Not only did he walk again; he joined the army and became a P.T.I. in the R.E.M.E., stationed at Borden in Hampshire with a heart as strong as a Lion. He has also attained 5th Dan Black Belts with instructor status in Shotokan Karate, Aikido, Korean Kempo and teaches Kick-boxing and Mixed Martial Arts in his spare time.

A writer since school, he has written several works of varying length, 'The Blackhawks Impossible Quest' being his first serious attempt at fantasy novel writing after taking a creative writing course. He has also written 'A Violent Man': the Time Travel novellas, 'All the Time in the World' and 'Time and Time Again', besides the children's novella: 'The Book, the Wand, the Magic'. He still resides in Sheffield where he ice skates almost every day at Ice Sheffield, particularly on Saturday and Sunday mornings amongst an array of treasured friends.

The Past is gone. The Present is here, now. The Future is a blank canvas that we can all paint on to make it our own!

Be careful, your whole life can change in a single defining moment!

There's more to time than the ticking of a clock. Pay attention only to the clock and you won't notice what others notice, and you won't know what others know!

M&E&B BOOKS
Second Edition

Printed in Dunstable, United Kingdom